JILL IS NOT HAPPY

JILL IS NOT HAPPY

KAIRA ROUDA

SCARLET
NEW YORK

JILL IS NOT HAPPY

Scarlet
An Imprint of Penzler Publishers
58 Warren Street
New York, N.Y. 10007

First Scarlet Press edition

Interior design by Maria Fernandez

Library of Congress Control Number: 2024949938

Hardcover ISBN: 978-1-61316-676-5
Paperback ISBN: 978-1-61316-607-9
eBook ISBN: 978-1-61316-608-6

10 9 8 7 6 5 4 3 2 1

Printed in the United States of America
Distributed by W. W. Norton & Company

To Harley.

Because of you, Kaira is happy.

Jack and Jill went up the hill
To fetch a pail of water
Jack fell down and broke his crown
And Jill came tumbling after

Jack got up, and home did trot
As fast as he could caper
Went to bed to mend his head
With vinegar and brown paper

Jill came in
And she did grin
To see his paper plaster;
Mother, vex'd
Did whip her next
For causing Jack's disaster

'Jack shall have Jill; / Nought shall go ill'

—Puck, *A Midsummer Night's Dream*

William Shakespeare

THEN

Tires screeched on the wet pavement and the car slid, careening to the right.

A flash of something in the headlights and then a terrible thud. Finally, the brakes held and the tires gripped the road again.

We stopped. Steam rose from the hood of the car. All around us was darkness, silence.

We both stepped out of the car and saw what we had done, illuminated in the headlights.

We had hit a person.

What were they doing on this dark, winding road?

This didn't happen, couldn't happen, but it did. Checked for a pulse. There was none.

We needed to go.

Pulled back onto the road. It was so late.

What could we possibly have done to help?

We needed to get home, get back to campus.

We needed to get out of there.

And we did.

PART ONE

UP A HILL

1

NOW

JILL

As I step into the busy coffee shop, my shoulders shoot to my ears. There are too many happy people in here. Happiness is an emotion I find to be as elusive as a consistent almond latte. There is always too much or too little milk, in my experience. Why can't anything be perfect? Jack and I used to be perfect, we were.

"Jill! Over here!" Michelle waves to me from a seat on the patio. I stand corrected. Michelle is perfect. She's wearing a canary-yellow dress, her auburn hair shiny and rolling over her shoulders. She looks like a ray of sunshine. It's good for someone like me to keep someone like Michelle as a friend; I realized that a long time ago when we were matched as freshman year roommates. It's important to have a best friend, and she is mine.

I push away my personal cloudbank and wave back at her, making my way to her table without acknowledging anyone else in the restaurant. I know some of them may recognize me, but I don't want to see them, or be seen by anyone except Jack. I never have.

Michelle pops up from her seat and wraps her arms around me in a hug. I do my best to imitate the gesture.

"So good to see you! I can't believe it's been a couple of months since we last grabbed coffee," she says, releasing me as we sit down together. "You've lost weight, haven't you? I mean, you look great, but you look thinner than usual. You must be stressed."

I smile. "You can never be too rich or too thin, right?" The weight loss is a byproduct of my life of late, not part of my plans. Some people eat when they're unhappy. I do the opposite.

"Tell me what's going on." Her face is a frown of concern. She's so darn nice. And earnest. I thought it was an act at first. It's not.

"You're the best. My best," I say. It's a refrain for a reason.

"I ordered you an almond latte, hope that's still your favorite?" Michelle says with a smile, pivoting.

"Perfect, you know I love those lattes." I smile back. "It's good to see you. I realize you're kept busy driving those boys of yours everywhere."

"It's hectic. But I need to make time for friends. It's so important." She pats my hand.

I don't like that she has many people in her life besides me, though Michelle doesn't know it. She just thinks I'm an introvert and so a long time ago stopped inviting me to group outings or even mentioning her other friends too much. It's the way I like it. Michelle and I have been friends since college, a time that seems like someone else's life. When I look back at photos of me then, I don't recognize myself. That Jill was so happy, and so very much in love. I mean, I still love Jack. It's just become complicated. I wonder how Michelle sees me now, besides thin.

"So how are the kids? How's Brad?" I ask.

Michelle's twins are fifteen years old and in high school. I don't envy her having two teen boys around. Can't imagine it. But I'm sure, for Michelle, every day is a blessing. If you take her word for it, most things are just wonderful. Of course, that's not true, but I'm certain she believes it to be.

"He worked so hard and finally it has paid off. He's graduated to a better schedule. He has so much more flexibility now, it's really wonderful. He gets to spend more time with the boys, and that's really such a blessing." Her eyes get a little misty thinking about her pilot husband, away at work in the sky. That's so sweet.

I look down at my wedding ring and spin it around my finger.

"How about you guys?" Michelle asks. "I saw Jack in town last week. It really is remarkable how he has kept his whole college looks. I mean, I love Brad to death, but he looks like a middle-aged man. Your Jack, well, he's still hot."

She is right about my genetically blessed husband, and I know she means her compliment innocently enough, so I keep a smile on my face. How about us? I can't tell her the truth. I wouldn't want to dash her image of Jack and me as the perfect couple, of course not. Michelle has been carrying that impression around since senior year of college. It was true then, and for a long time after. Now, we'll see. Every couple has rough patches, but there is no need to tell the world about them. Best to handle things privately. I'll fix us. I always do.

"Jack and I are having a lot of fun empty nesting." I grin. "There's nobody there to bother us when the moment strikes. Maybe that's my weight loss plan?"

"Oh my gosh. Lucky you. So you're just having sex all the time?" Michelle's eyes are wide trying to imagine it, along with an empty house.

"All the time," I say. "Now that Maggie's in college, well, it's almost like we're newlyweds again."

"I guess there's an upside for when the boys go to college. But I'm still dreading the thought of an empty nest."

"Oh, you shouldn't. It's wonderful. Maggie is in her happy place, living her best life. And so are we," I say with a smile. That I only know this from social media is a fact I keep to myself. My daughter and I, well, we struggle to connect.

"And how's Jack? I realize he had a big disappointment with the election."

Jack was mayor of our town for a couple of years. He did love it, but then he lost in the last election, in a rather scandalous manner, unfortunately.

"He's fine. Just needs to figure out his next act, you know?" I answer as the waitress places my drink in front of me. "I mean, he is a little, um . . ." I struggle to find the right word.

Michelle reaches across the table for my hand. "Honey, what is it?"

I wait for the waitress to walk past us with a plate of eggs and sausage, and my stomach growls. I do need to remember to eat.

"The truth is, Jack's depressed. I don't know if it's the election or something else. Even though he looks the same on the outside, let's just say, he's not the Jack I fell in love with. He tries, he does, but it seems like one of the only places we're connecting right now is the bedroom."

"Oh, dear, I'm so sorry. What can I do?" Michelle asks.

"Nothing. He'll have to tackle this himself, with my help," I answer.

"Depression is serious, Jill. The number of calls to suicide hotlines is skyrocketing."

Yes, I know. I allow a tear to spill over onto my cheek before quickly swiping at it with my napkin. "Oh, it's not that bad, really, he just needs to figure out what's next and then I'm sure he'll be fine," I say. "I'm helping him every step of the way. Don't worry."

Michelle's happy face falls with concern. She nods doubtfully. I feel bad about that, I really do.

"We're finally going to take that road trip to Utah's national parks," I say. "We leave in the morning."

"You've been talking about getting away for a while. A trip is the perfect solution. Get out of the rut of being at home and get outside." Michelle nods vigorously, brightening again. "When we snuck away to Big Sur last winter, it was life-changing. You never know how much stress and worry you're holding until you get away. My neck had been so tense and now, look, I can turn it again." She demonstrates, her brown hair spinning across her shoulders.

"Yes, it will be lovely to get away," I say.

"I mean, in Big Sur, we finally had sex again without teenage boys around." She takes a sip of coffee. "I need to go back."

I smile at my friend, and she pats my hand.

"Well, it should help lighten Jack's mood. Sunshine, fresh air. Nothing better. I'm excited to hike and talk, to reconnect outside the bedroom."

"I'm sure it will be just what the doctor ordered. You always have been the golden couple," she says. "Like a fairy tale." I love that she sees the best, the brightest, in people.

Even when she shouldn't.

"Jack and Jill is a nursery rhyme," I remind her. "Not a fairy tale."

"Same same," she says. All's well, or will be, she's decided, despite Jack's election loss and subsequent bout of depression. I'm certain she'll tell her husband about that. Jack Tingley has never before had anything to be sad about, as far as most people are concerned. That's good gossip.

"I better get going. A lot of packing to do," I say. "I haven't been hiking for years, or to a national park. Neither has Jack."

"You'll love it," Michelle says. "Go on, I'll get the check. And I'll expect to hear all about it when you get back. Have some romance for me."

"Oh, don't worry, we will." I blow her a kiss and hurry out of the café, pleased with myself. Experts say you should tell someone where you're going when you're heading out into the wilderness in case you get lost or into trouble.

In case you need to be rescued. We're good at getting ourselves out of trouble as long as we stick together. That's the part I'm worried about though.

The togetherness.

2
NOW

———

JILL

Jack and I live in what can only be described as a charming home—Cape Cod style, well landscaped, perfectly maintained—on a desirable yet non-pretentious suburban street in a gated community in our otherwise too affluent town. I pull my Audi into the garage and push the button to drop the door, surrounding myself in silence, then take a deep breath and a moment to be thankful. We own this home outright. That piece of good luck is about the only thing we've had going for us financially for years.

I could be envious of my neighbors, the grandness of their homes, the newness of their cars, the jet-setting nature of their social media feeds. Jack's mayoral campaigns resulted in speaking gigs at a number of sprawling mansions and elegant hideaways in town. Some homes so unbelievably large I would have thought they were hotels had I not been invited inside as the trailing spouse. We will never be that rich, or that lucky. At this point, we barely hold onto what we have.

But I've learned to let all that go and appreciate what we have. And what we do have is built on stories. Mine as a freelance writer, Jack's as a skilled communicator both with his own small law firm and as a politician. Everyone at the magazine loved hearing my stories from the campaign trail. Gossip, political gossip, is a welcome reprieve from glossy stories of new restaurant openings and black-tie events. All that changed when Jack lost the election. I don't have much insider scoop anymore, not that the others at the magazine would care about, not really.

"Hey!" Jack knocks on my car window, and I scream.

I'm shaking all over as I open the car door. "What the hell?"

"Good morning to you too," he says, dark eyes flashing, cheek dimple hiding. "Why are you sitting in the dark in the garage?" He pulls open my car door and extends his hand.

Some people like to think, to reflect. Some people like to be alone, to contemplate. Not Jack. I place my hand in his and welcome the familiar zing of attraction that zips through my body. While I'd like to act on that, I'm still mad he snuck up on me.

"I was meditating, ok? You should try it sometime," I say, dropping his hand and pushing past him as I head into the house. I feel Jack following behind me.

"Look, I'm sorry I scared you." He touches my shoulder, and another ping rushes through me.

I turn and meet his eyes. I doubt he's sorry.

Michelle is right about my husband. Jack looks much like he did twenty years ago, with only a sprinkle of gray at his temples, dark hair, square jaw, unnerving eyes. Jack likes surprises, spontaneity, and other adrenaline-inducing things. Before, when we were newly married, his surprises would be romantic: a special date night to a hidden beach complete with a picnic, flowers for no reason, and after Maggie was born, a beautiful necklace commemorating her arrival.

Those were lovely days, happier times, times when we knew the future was a sparkling world of possibilities. A future like the one Michelle believed in and has achieved. Jack hung his shingle out and started his own law practice. His parents revealed the trust fund that eventually allowed us to buy this home, free and clear. I loved my freelance writing career, taking projects I wanted to take, not working because I had to like now.

Those were the best of days. Now, the weight of the world, and the past, has taken its toll on us.

"It's fine, Jack, but you knew exactly what you were doing. You always have."

"True," he says with a grin. "And you're still really cute when you're angry."

I shake my head and put my purse down on the kitchen island and pick up the packing list I printed from an article online. "Are you packed?"

I feel his arms wrap around my waist, his lips brush my neck. "I've been thinking, maybe we should bag the trip, stay around here. I might have a job interview come up." He moves away before I can respond and walks toward the refrigerator so I can't see his bullshit face. The law firm isn't doing well, and Jack needs another job, he's decided. His heart was never into being an attorney; he became one because it was what his parents wanted for him. Jack always was easily swayed by those he loved.

"We're going. The lodges are booked. I've spent hours planning this trip," I say. That's true. More time than he could imagine. Not that he would.

"Well, here's to us, just the two of us, on a vacation, I guess," he says. "When's the last time we tried this? I can't even remember."

"Our honeymoon," I say and busy myself rummaging in my purse.

"You're kidding."

"I'm not." I look up at my husband of twenty-two years.

"We went on the trip to Cabo with Michelle and Brad."

"Yes, we did." I really don't want to talk about all the things we haven't done, so I cross the kitchen to the white ceramic farm sink, a designer highlight of the space I'm quite proud of, still. After I turn on the faucet and fill a glass with water, I take a sip and watch Jack squirm.

"We went with Maggie's class to Disney. Oh, and to Paris," he says. "And what about that time we visited my parents before they died? That was just the two of us."

"A trip to their second home in Palm Desert in August?"

He shrugs. "At least it was something."

I stare at him. He knows that trip to the desert doesn't count. And as far as reconnecting, it didn't work. His parents were the opposite of welcoming, the epitome of judging, especially his mom. We should have at least been given the

Palm Desert house when they died, but nope. Almost every-thing went to charity. "We're going to Utah."

"We're going to Utah," he mimics. "Whether we like it or not."

I smile as my husband stomps out of the kitchen like a baby. He should be careful, but he doesn't realize that yet. He's taken to pushing me a bit too much since Maggie left for college. He's had the freedom to be more himself, I suppose, without her watching, adoring eyes.

With the daddy's girl safely tucked away in Santa Cruz, Daddy has turned back into Jack. I would just like to be sure he turns into the Jack I fell in love with in college, the Jack who is the love of my life. Not someone else.

3
NOW

JILL

I am in my closet—blissfully we each have our own walk-in—choosing the perfect hiking attire. I've spent a few weeks shopping online, with boxes arriving almost every day, and I'm going to look good despite the looming credit card balance my hiking fashion has created. I'll handle that little issue later. My goal is to dress so Jack will notice me again.

"Make sure you pack a pullover or a vest. It's cold at night, especially in Bryce Canyon."

Jack can hear me, even in his closet, but as I wait for the response, I also know it likely won't come. He's tuned me out since our little argument of sorts in the kitchen. That's fine. It's part of our pattern. A pattern my therapist Dr. Kline knows I've been trying to break. It's tough to do it alone though. And Jack won't agree to couples' counseling, I recognize that. I haven't even bothered to ask.

During my last session Dr. Kline asked me to say how happy I am in my marriage on a scale of one to ten. I told him an eight, but that's a lie right now. Jack's attention has drifted and that drives me crazy. When he asked me to rate how satisfied I was with our sex life, I told him it was a ten. That's sort of true. We have a sizzling physical attraction between us, we do. We just need to act on it more. We will this weekend.

One might wonder why I choose to stay in this relationship of ours. We do seem, what's the word . . . stuck, I suppose. Well, I'm comfortable here, with Jack. He is the only man I've ever loved, or ever will love.

When I look at him, I see us young, and happy. I see what was and that's enough for me. I'll never forget the first time he noticed me, smiled at me with that dimpled grin. The energy pulsing between us still is something I could never replace, and never want to. We are bonded on a molecular level. Sometimes, I know, it isn't enough for him. We can't all live in a world of our own making. But I can. I will make him love this world of ours again too.

That's why we need a little trip. A reset. A spring break, so to speak. Our March road trip. A chance to set things straight, remember the rules and promises.

I finish packing and head downstairs to the kitchen. For our last supper at home, I want to prepare something special. Something hearty and comforting. I glance outside at my hydroponic garden bursting with greens. It's a vertical tower with six plants per level, six levels high. Once a week, I add nutrients and check the pH levels. I order new seedlings for my tower once I've harvested as much as I can. I've also taken to growing my own herbs and greens from scratch. I love to add flowers to my salads. Bright yellow and orange marigolds burst from the top of my tower, while at the bottom, a winding vine with white trumpet-shaped flowers makes a pretty, social media worthy photo, not that I'm a fan of social media. I'm on there, but only to look at other's posts. A voyeur. I'd never share my life.

I trot outside to the tower, pull a leaf of oregano, and chew it while I examine the rest of the potential harvest. I decide we'll have a salad from the garden for dinner, with some sort of baked fish on the side. I know I have salmon in the freezer. I grab my garden scissors and snip off some dark green Toscano kale, light green romaine, a few basil leaves, some crisp bok choy, colorful tatsoi, and some marigolds, and the white trumpets. The assortment with the flowers on top looks beautiful in the bowl.

It's always a special treat to eat something prepared with love. I'm certain Jack will appreciate the gesture.

4
THEN

JILL

'd been at USC for three years. Three long years of looking for Mr. Right. Well, correction, I had a list of potential partners, literally, taped to my dorm room wall. I started freshman year, the year the universe gave me Michelle Younkin as my roommate and best friend.

My life would be complete once I found him. I'd been working my way down the list since second half of freshman year. Despite Michelle's teasing.

"This isn't how you find true love, you know," Michelle said for the hundredth time. "This is a fantasy. You don't even know these guys."

"But I know what I'm looking for," I said and rolled over on my bed. "The right guy isn't easy to find. I am looking for someone stable and fun and handsome. I don't have anyone,

Michelle, well, except you. I need a guy I can rely on. A life partner. I'm tired of being alone."

"You'll always have me, but I get it, I do." She paused to think. "It's just a weird way to go about things."

"You've never had to face the world on your own. My list wouldn't seem so strange if you had," I told her.

I watched her eyes fill with tears, and she gave me a big hug. "You'll find Mr. Right and I'll make sure of it."

"Thank you," I said.

Michelle didn't know it, but I had a date with Number 2 on my list that evening. I felt smug, powerful. I'd find my man and then make him fall for me.

By the beginning of senior year, I'd been on at least one date with all the top seven men on my list and had crossed them out of contention. The reasons they were cut from the list were varied, but after one date, I could tell. The guys were too boring, or too self-absorbed. One guy spent our entire date talking about who he was going out with the next night. One of them made me so angry boasting about his family and their wealth that I had to walk out before dinner was over. He made me feel so insignificant, disposable.

I was down to Jack Tingley, number eight. Of the Tingley family of Bel Air. President of his fraternity, handsome, not a care in the world because he'd go on to join the family law firm and make millions. I'd been trying to get his attention at parties on fraternity row for years, with no luck. Tonight had to be different.

Michelle and I dressed in our tightest party clothes. She ditched her boyfriend, Brad, and told him we'd see him later. She was on my mission with me. So, there we stood, as we had many times in the past, on the front porch of Jack's fraternity, when I saw him. And he finally saw me. Michelle pushed me toward him and disappeared into the party.

"I haven't seen you here before," a drunk Jack whispered in my ear. I'd been to the Friday night parties his fraternity hosted every week since our freshman year. For him to see me now, years later, well, it was a bit frustrating, I'll admit. But, finally, at least he saw me. "I'm Jack Tingley. President of this little fraternity here."

"I'm Jill Larkin and it's my first time coming here," I answered with a lie and touched his shoulder. "Is it always so loud?"

"Yes. But I know a place that's not. Come with me." He took my hand and we walked away from the party, down the street, and to a home he shared with two other guys who were back at the party. I'd seen the house, from outside, of course. It was nothing like what I could afford, and everyone gossiped about the guys who had the privilege to live in the grand old house on fraternity row.

And now, I'd be able to say I'd been inside. I remember my heart racing with fear. Would Jack flip on bright lights and realize I wasn't what he thought he saw? But as we stepped inside the door, he turned on an overhead chandelier and escorted me to a lovely seating area. I was alone with Jack Tingley.

"You're beautiful," he said, handing me a glass of wine in an actual wineglass. "I can't believe we haven't met. Have you been here all four years?"

"Thank you, yes, I'm a senior like you." I blushed, trying to keep my excitement under control.

"Well, cheers, Jill, to finally meeting. Let me show you around the house. It's special, lots of history. Then we could go grab something to eat?"

"That sounds great." It took everything in me not to jump for joy. I could feel the attraction zipping between us. Jack Tingley liked me. He really did.

And he was everything I'd been looking for wrapped into a handsome package: polite, with a great sense of humor, and he asked questions about me and really listened. He was mature, and sure of himself, but not at all boastful. He seemed to have a big heart. I was in love with him. At first sight. Well, at first sight that he knew about. And I knew from that evening forward we were meant to be together.

Forever.

When I came home that night, glowing, Michelle was up waiting for me. "So? What happened? Did he take you out?"

I fell onto the bed, stars in my eyes. "Yes, and we talked, and laughed. He's so nice, genuine. I'm in love."

"I cannot believe this. You actually went on a date, and had fun, with a guy on your list. It's about time," Michelle said. "So, what happens next?"

"What do you mean?" I asked.

"I mean, do you move on to number nine or see Jack for a bit?"

"Oh, no, I'm finished with the list. I'm marrying Jack. By the end of the year, or sooner." I held up my left hand and imagined a large engagement ring sparkling there.

"Knowing you, you'll make it happen."

"I'm so happy," I said. "And you'll be my maid of honor, of course."

I know she wanted to laugh because I was planning my wedding to the guy I'd just had a first date with, but Michelle is a good, kind person, so she simply smiled. She could tell from the tone of my voice I was quite serious.

"I'd be honored, Jill," she said.

And everything was set, for the rest of my life.

5
NOW

JILL

I'm lighting the white taper candles when Jack walks into the kitchen.

"Whoa, what's the special occasion? It's not our anniversary." Then he adds, "Right?"

I shoot him a look.

"Jilly, I'm kidding," he says and kisses me on the cheek.

"It's our last dinner."

"What? Really?"

"I mean, it's our last dinner together at home for a while," I say and shift the crystal candle holders to the center of the table. I've set the table with our wedding china and stemware, which must be the reason Jack mentioned our anniversary. "We were married in May. It's only March. But these are from our registry. What a wonderful day that was."

Twenty-one years ago, we'd had a huge wedding with 350 guests, hosted and paid for by Jack's parents at their sprawling winery in Paso Robles, although his mom had always wanted to host it at their home in Bel Air. But things change. Every moment of our wedding was perfect, from the farm-to-table food to the free-flowing champagne. I still could not believe I was marrying Jack Tingley. I'd hit the jackpot, so to speak. I look at my husband now, and he does not seem to be sharing the same happy memories.

"Wasn't the wedding wonderful, Jack?" I ask, trying to snap him out of his trance. He's staring at the flickering candlelight. "Last year's anniversary, well, we should have tried harder."

"Uh huh," Jack says, still distracted.

Last year's anniversary was unremarkable, for sure. We'd only shared a perfunctory dinner out at a chain restaurant and exchanged a couple small gifts—it's brass and nickel for the twenty-first, of all things. I gave him a paperweight, and he gave me a letter opener. But in our defense, Maggie was home from boarding school, and well, when Maggie is around, she is the center of our world, anniversary or not. Of course, as it should be.

"What are you thinking about?" I ask before walking back into the kitchen to finish preparing dinner.

"How much I don't want to go on a road trip to Utah," Jack says and then finds something fascinating to stare at on the floor. He looks up again. "I'm sorry, I just, I really don't. It's not you, it's me."

I turn around and continue tossing the salad in my home-made dressing: pepper, salt, olive oil, freshly squeezed lemon juice. I don't like it when Jack whines like this. I don't. And yes, I agree, it is all your fault, Jack.

I drop the salad tongs on the marble counter. Perhaps I hit them on the counter. I don't know. Jack jumps.

"The trip is planned. You agreed to it weeks ago. We will have fun. We will reconnect. We need to reconnect." I turn back to tossing the salad.

Jack pulls a chair from the table and sits, elbows on the table, staring at me. "What if I don't want to reconnect?"

I shake my head. "Well, that's just not an option, darling. We are due for some romantic hikes in the wilderness. I'm even going to write a piece for the magazine about our little adventure. You know how I like to write about us and our connection. Did you know that the skies in Utah, in some of these national parks, have the best stargazing in the world?"

I watch as Jack swallows whatever it is he'd like to say. And then he replaces those words with "No, I didn't know that. Ok, well, it sounds like fun. Despite everything, I do like being with you."

"See, that's the spirit. It will be great. Dinner's almost ready. Would you like to pick some wine? We're having lemon and herb encrusted salmon. Doesn't it smell wonderful?"

I hear the chair scrape against the wood floor as he pushes away from the table, but I don't watch Jack walk to the wine fridge. I don't need to.

He's back on track.

6
NOW

JILL

'm plating the fish, garnishing our meals with the fresh thyme from my hydroponic tower. I enjoy the art of this, the color of the pink fish on the white plate, the sprig of thyme, the slice of lemon.

I jump as Jack wraps his arm around my waist. "You scared me."

"You love surprises," Jack says and nibbles on my neck. "I hope red is ok? Even though it's fish?"

He holds the bottle out in front of both of us.

"It's from your parents' wine cellar, isn't it?" I note the red dot affixed to the bottle.

His parents deployed a color-coding system in their wine collection. Green dots meant fine to drink every day, yellow a bit more expensive. The red dots were for the best bottles in their cellar. Lucky for us, the collection was housed offsite at a special company with a huge wine cellar where they rent space. Fortunately, we have the key. We can enjoy a red dot wine whenever we'd like, and we often do.

I thought we'd be left with much more than a wine collection from his wealthy parents' estate when they died, but it didn't turn out that way. I tamp down the anger that always appears when I think of the fortune we never received and force a smile.

"Oh, a special bottle too. It will be lovely."

Jack releases his hold on me, and I'm reminded of his physical strength and the way he can still make my heart skip a beat. He played intermural sports in college, and he's worked hard to keep in shape ever since.

"I'll decant the wine," he says, walking away. "Oh, and Jill?"

"Yes?"

"No salad for me tonight. I didn't feel great after last night's meal. Something in there, well, anyway, I'm sticking to iceberg lettuce from now on." Jack pats his six-pack stomach and reaches for the decanter.

Fine. I scrape his salad onto my plate and wipe the dressing residue from his. The presentation isn't quite the same, but it will have to do for now. I carry the plates to the table and take my seat.

"I'm sure it wasn't my homegrown lettuce that upset your stomach," I say, watching as he pours the red wine into my glass. "It must be something else."

"Better safe than sorry." Jack pours wine for himself and takes the seat across from me. "Oh, you're wearing the necklace tonight. Looks nice."

I touch the stone nestled at the base of my neck. A flawless emerald-cut diamond, surrounded by sapphire baguettes. A special piece. He does always seem startled to see it, and I enjoy the reaction. "Thank you. I thought I'd wear something special tonight. Remind us of all we have achieved. Together. Cheers!"

We clink wineglasses, and I think Jack's smile is genuine, despite the fit he pitched over the necklace several years ago. I guess it has grown on him. I take a sip of the expensive wine and watch my husband.

"Why are you staring at me?" Jack asks while chewing. "The fish is good."

"I was wondering if you've changed your mind. If maybe you're excited to see the hoodoos and arches."

"I know you've worked hard to plan the trip, so I have decided to try to enjoy it." He pushes his mouth into a smile. There's the dimple. "Is that satisfactory?"

"We can have some fun along the way." I watch his face drop.

"No, we can't. This is only a road trip. Nothing more."

He hasn't wanted to have fun in a very long time. I touch the necklace again and draw his attention. "Please. Don't tell me you don't get a rush from it. You still remember the first time, I know you do."

"No, Jill," he says. But I see the twinkle in his eye. He remembers the thrill of it, reaching his hand into his suit jacket pocket and finding the necklace there. "That little skill of yours. Did you learn it from your parents, or did it just come naturally?"

"Oh, no, not my parents. I am the original argument for nature over nurture," I say, and that much is true. I've had to make my own way for a long time, my own fun, my own future. And it all centers around Jack. He's my world.

"You're funny, Jilly, that's for sure." Jack laughs and I love the sound. I see his dimple. He's remembering how it felt, and we'll have fun doing it again, but I won't push it right now. I hold my tongue. He knows it really isn't up to him.

"So, what is the promising job lead you have?" He's been home, doing nothing but playing golf and pretending to own a law firm, for almost a year. When he was mayor, business at the firm was booming. People like to be associated with winners, and Jack was busier than ever fulfilling his mayor duties and keeping his burgeoning client base happy. Since the scandal, well, most of the new business left, along with Jack's clients. It's hard to trust a lawyer embroiled in such a mess, I suppose. His partner Tony's clients are keeping the rent paid, the doors open. We've been relying on our savings ever since. My meager salary from the magazine barely covers a week of groceries a month. But I write because I must. Jack is in charge of keeping us in the lifestyle to which we've become accustomed. A very nice and very expensive lifestyle, I'll admit.

"I'm being considered for general manager at the country club, actually."

Well, that is a genuine surprise. "Really? How did that come about?"

"You know, just networking," he says. He refills each of our glasses, draining the bottle. "I think I'd be good at it. It's a big opportunity."

"The Club has been good to us," I agree. "It's bursting with opportunities."

"Glad you approve." I watch Jack extract another red dot red bottle from our wine cooler—this one a cabernet, which will overpower the meal—and think about the possibilities at The Club. It's one of the most exclusive and priciest in Southern California, with a waiting list fifteen years long, last I asked.

Would Jack being a manager diminish our sparkle in the eyes of all those people, those neighbors?

What would Michelle think? I don't suppose it really matters, but it does give me pause. Jack has made a plan. Jack has been talking about his future, but with who? Not me, that's for sure.

"So, have you actually interviewed?" I ask him as he pours the contents of the new bottle into the decanter. He is celebrating something tonight.

"It's not really like that. I've spoken to the executive director. Stanley Duncan. He approached me, confidentially," he says, filling my wineglass.

"No one knows about this except the executive director?"

"No, I haven't told Tony or any of the guys. I guess I wanted to see your reaction, clear it with you. You do understand the potential, right?" Jack sits down and takes a sip of wine.

"I do." I'll admit this new development has me thinking. But my plans are set. "But we're still going on our trip. You haven't committed to anything, right?"

"I told Stanley I'd talk it over with you and get back to him as soon as possible." He's excited about the job. It's written all over his face. It's almost as if he's already said yes.

"Why haven't you told me about this? Why did you keep it a secret? We are a team, remember?" I know I might have what Jack calls my "scary" tone of voice. It's not scary, it's just disappointment. A disappointed voice.

"I wanted to surprise you," he says. "Surprise!"

I take a sip of wine and watch my handsome husband. "And no one else knows about this?"

"Just Maggie. We talked this morning, and she loves the idea."

I can't help but shake my head. Of course he told our daughter before he told me. She is his sun and moon. She is his security blanket too, or so he thinks. "And what did Marvelous Maggie say exactly?"

Jack shrugs. "She said you would tell me not to do it because it wouldn't look good socially. And because I want to do it. She's just trying to look out for me."

I roll my eyes.

"We both know you two have your issues."

Issues you've done your best to exploit so you could come between us. "You created the daddy's girl, Jack. You did it. Did you tell her about our road trip?"

"No, actually, but I'll call her tomorrow from the road. I guess I'll wait until next week to move on."

Interesting choice of words. "Move on?"

"You know, with my career."

"Right," I say and finish my glass of wine. It's a rich, bold wine, and it matches Jack's mood. "Refill please."

Jack fills my glass without saying another word, smug in the knowledge he kept a secret from me. When will he ever learn?

7
NOW

JILL

I leave Jack to do the dishes and stomp upstairs. I don't love it when they gang up on me. I think about my daughter, and a cloud of red-hot anger fills my mind. How dare Jack tell her about his job offer before me? How dare they conspire against me?

I should have handled this issue a long time ago. I should have put a stop to their tight relationship or at least ensure a balanced one for Maggie and me. But I didn't. Frankly, I didn't really care. I know that sounds terrible, but here's the thing: you can pick your friends, but you can't pick your family. Almost from the moment she arrived, she'd reach for Jack over me. And as soon as she was bottle feeding, it was only Jack who could comfort her.

Did she sense something in me that pushed her away? Who knows? I am still her mother. That is supposed to come with respect and unconditional love, although I must admit, I didn't show that kind of respect to my own parents. So I guess, in Maggie's case, she treats her mom like I treated mine. She doesn't love me like she should. She saves her love for Jack and her many friends.

Maggie is my opposite, that is true. She moves through the world surrounded by big groups of people and laughter. She would never have just one best friend like I do with Michelle. Michelle is my friend because I needed a role model, someone who is kind and loving, someone who would become a good wife and mother. What Michelle sees in me is a reflection of herself. She believes I'm as wonderful as she is, and she's inadvertently helped me learn to pretend to be so when I want to. Michelle has been my teacher since freshman year in college, and well, she's invaluable.

Maggie would find having only one friend *limiting*—her word—and her world, her future, is limitless, she tells us. Maybe she's right, or maybe she just hasn't faced reality yet. In an instant, everything can change. And she hasn't had one of those bad instants yet. Her young life has been blissful and tragedy free. Except for losing her grandparents on her father's side, she hasn't known loss.

The world has a way of catching up with people like my daughter. She'll find that out, soon, I suspect.

Jack walks into our bedroom. "What time do you want to leave tomorrow?"

We both glaze over our argument from dinner like professional bakers icing a cake. There are so many layers of unfinished disagreements in the cake we're baking. What will happen when we don't have any more room in the pan, I wonder.

"Early bird catches the worm and misses rush hour," I say.

"I can't start driving that early. Let's do this. We'll leave around 10:00 a.m. I mapped it. It's a seven-hour drive to Zion National Park. We'll be there by five in the afternoon or so. Gives me time for a quick workout at The Club," Jack says as he pushes his hair from his forehead. A nervous habit.

"Sure. Sounds great." I reach for the necklace around my neck, grab the pendant, and yank hard. I feel a surge of relief as the chain falls to the bedroom floor. "And we will have some fun along the way."

Jack takes a step back, and then another. He shakes his head. "No, *we* definitely won't. See you in the morning, Jill. Get some sleep."

He pulls my bedroom door closed and heads to his room down the hall past Maggie's bedroom, to the guest room. It's now Jack's bedroom. It's humiliating that he doesn't want to share a bedroom with me anymore. It's been like this for six weeks, yet I am powerless to lure him back to me. I've tried everything I know. I even started going to counseling, although I find it too embarrassing to tell Dr. Kline the whole truth. I need insights from someone, that's a fact. I need help. Jack says he just can't make love to me right now, not with everything that's happened. He's been drifting away from me since Maggie left for college. Moving down the hall to sleep, well, that's unacceptable.

And unsustainable, he'll realize soon. Everything that's happened has been because of both of us, of our dreams, our goals, our secrets. I happen to know there is more than a quick workout awaiting him tomorrow morning.

Why is he allowed to step outside the marriage when I am so devoted to it? The answer is: He's not.

8

NOW

JACK

Erica's house, the one she was awarded in the divorce settlement last month, sits on the edge of a cliff on the edge of the Pacific Ocean. It's contemporary, filled with art and colorful furnishings. It's sunny and bright, like Erica herself.

We made love this morning as soon as I arrived and watched the sunrise together from her oversized master bedroom. I showered first, and now, as I wait in the front courtyard for her to appear, I think about my life with my wife.

We share, loosely, a cramped Cape Cod that my parents paid for, the same house for more than twenty years. We never moved up, but at least we didn't slip behind. We should have, of course, but we got creative. Had some fun, Jill would say.

The fun is over. I've made up my mind. I'm getting a job, a real, reputable position with The Club. Sure, it will turn some heads because I'll be employed by my friends. But it's all in the way you handle things, and that social perception situation, I can handle.

It's Jill who I cannot handle. Sure, she's sexy as hell, and a lot of fun when she wants to be. She still looks like the coed I met all those years ago on the porch of the fraternity house, she really does. Blonde hair, in-shape body, and huge, ice-blue eyes. People who meet her never forget her. From the moment I met her, I knew she was trouble. But I was smitten, and then fate brought us together for life. That's what I've always believed. But now, with Maggie off to college and a new job offer, I am beginning to see a future without Jill. I need to get away from her to save myself, I can feel it. I have never been able to imagine it would be possible before now.

That's why I'm here, with Erica. She's calm and thoughtful, patient, and kind. That might sound boring to any other person, but to me, she's the answer to my dependence on Jill. Erica is the only way I'll break the habit.

Erica appears, dashing out the glass front door wearing a flowing white dress and a big smile. A real smile. Her long dark hair is pulled up into a high ponytail. Her lips shimmer in the morning sunshine. She reaches my side and wraps both arms around my neck.

"Sorry to keep you waiting," she whispers before kissing me.

Every one of my senses is on fire. She smells like flowers in the spring, and the way her body folds into mine is refreshing, sensual. Erica is soft, and Jill is hard, edgy. I know I shouldn't make the comparison, but I do.

I pull away from our embrace, holding her hands in mine. "I hate to tell you this, but I am going to go on the Utah trip. It's complicated, but I need to do it."

"So this is why you had to go for a drive with me this morning? To tell me you're going on vacation with your wife?" Erica pulls her hands away so they can land on her hips. "I really can't believe this. You told me you were over."

I take a deep breath. "We are. But it's not finished. I need to be finished. A clean break. This trip will give me that closure. It will give me a chance to talk it through with Jill. I owe her that much after all these years."

Erica's frown softens, just a little, but her hands stay on her hips. "Look, I know you've been together for a long time. There's history and all that. Memories. Dean and I were together ten years, half the time you two, and it was still bittersweet. Especially for him when I took the house." She smiles. "But things got ugly fast. You know that. I told you I had to get a restraining order. I don't know what good a lot of talking will do. Take it from me, when it's over, it's over."

I pull her into my arms. "I want to be with you. Live with you in your stolen house. And we will. Just give me this last trip. Trust me, I need to talk to her. Come on, let's go grab breakfast."

I open the door of my black SUV for Erica while a warning light goes off in my brain. Will Jill smell another woman's presence, her perfume, on my car's leather seat? I decide I'll drive through the car wash on the way home and ask them to spray deodorizer, infuse the car with fake pine scent. As I climb behind the wheel, I've calmed down.

Jill has me on edge. I need these last few moments with a normal woman to get centered and relax before the long drive to Utah.

"Jack, what is it?" Erica stares at me, and I wonder how long I've drifted.

"Nothing. We're all set." I force a smile as we drive through the gates at the end of her driveway. She lives in a guarded community and has her own additional security for her house. We are safe here, I remind myself. Safe and private, away from prying eyes. I can already imagine moving in here. I take a deep breath.

It's still early, 7:45 a.m. I decide we'll go to the serve your-self health food store we both love for the strong coffee and healthy ingredients. I'll have Erica back home by 8:30 a.m. I'll drive to the car wash, slip him a big tip for a quick turn-around, and be home by 9:00 a.m. We'll load up the car and hit the road right at 10:00 a.m. as promised.

I'm a man of my word. I have been all these years. Until Erica, I've been faithful too. I will explain my plan to Jill. She won't like it, not at first, but she will agree it's the only path forward. We've had a good run. We share so many secrets.

Without her, I don't think I'd be where I am today. I know I wouldn't be. But that was twenty-one years ago. Since then, everything we've done, we've done together within the cover of our marriage. As a team. I swallow. Jill has to feel the same way, she has to. Maybe, just maybe, she'll welcome a fresh start of her own.

"What now? You look like you tasted something rotten," Erica says. She puts her hand on my thigh.

"No, I'm fine. Still a little queasy from that dinner the other night."

"You said you had a salad, right? Salads don't usually make you sick unless it's salmonella or something. Didn't you have salmon that night? Ooh, do you have salmonella?" Erica's eyes are wide and she pulls her hand away. "Maybe Jill is trying to poison you? Like in the movies? I don't know what she looks like, and I don't want to, but does she have a sinister smile? Or, like one of those evil chuckles?"

She's so cute. "No, Jill is just a regular person, and our relationship has run its course, as you know. And no, salmon doesn't cause salmonella poisoning. A bacterium from feces causes that. And Jill wouldn't try to poison me."

I turn into the restaurant parking lot and check my watch. Right on time.

"Don't you think she knows you want out?" Erica asks as we walk through the parking lot.

"Well, I don't know. I think Jill only thinks about Jill. But things have gotten more tense since I moved to the guest room. Per your request." I kiss Erica on the cheek and keep her close. "This weekend will give me a chance to tell her everything. Promise. And I'm going to ask for an amicable divorce."

My mind flashes back to the last argument Jill and I had a few days ago. She was insistent that we go on the trip to Utah, and I'd finally relented. To keep the peace for a few more days and to make some plans. I needed to explain everything to Maggie too. Telling Jill the truth, away from our usual routine, to explain to her why we'd both be better off apart. This seemed like a good idea. I'd just walked in the door, and she confronted me in the entry hall.

"So you're finally agreeing to the trip?" Jill had asked, her voice taut with anger. We stood in the foyer, my hand on the doorknob, and I'd fought the urge to just walk back out. I knew, though, that wasn't a possibility. We needed to reach an understanding.

I took a deep breath and stared at my wife. "Yes, Jill, I've decided I'll go on the road trip with you. It will give us a chance to talk," I said.

"Talk and reconnect," Jill said before turning on her heels and leaving me alone in the hallway.

"This is the last time I'm letting you go on vacation with her," Erica says as we wait in line, pulling me back to the present.

I scan the people in the restaurant, just to be sure no one I know is in here. It's a younger crowd, high school kids and surfers. No one I know, or who knows me.

"This is the last time I am going to be with her, period. Don't worry." I check my watch. "Would it be ok to get this to go? We stayed in bed a little longer than I planned."

"Sure." Erica smiles. She's beautiful in a wholesome, regular person way. Nobody stares at her when she walks into a restaurant, and that's good. Can I keep this? Can I have this? A relationship built on attraction, yes, but also ease and true friendship. And then my thoughts leap to Jill. My heart skips a beat as dread bubbles up like boiling water. Jill and I were forced together by situations outside our control, but somehow Jill has always called the shots. With Erica, we are equals. It's so foreign I almost don't believe it could be true.

At least, not for me.

9
NOW

JILL

I stomp my feet to dislodge the last of the sand and dirt from my hiking boots. I had a spontaneous notion this morning to go on a hike down to the ocean. I'll be sitting, riding in the car, for the rest of the day. And you know what they say: Sitting is the new smoking. I always did love a good cigarette, back when not everyone glared at you like a felon. Back when you could smoke carefree and innocently. E-cigs aren't anything like the real thing.

I'm still savoring the memory of the deep inhale of my cigarette, a Virginia Slim, when a cough escapes my chest. Clearly, my lungs aren't used to this any longer. I smell my fingers and pick up the telltale whiff of smoke, so I hurry inside to wash my hands. Truth be told, I'm a closet smoker, a very infrequent closet smoker. This morning, awakened by Jack's early departure, it felt like the perfect morning to come out of the closet, so to speak, and enjoy a cigarette at sunrise. I'm not ashamed I did it. There was nobody around to judge me, and I'll eliminate the incriminating evidence on my hands before Jack returns from his workout.

I've already tossed the cigarettes and the lighter in a public trash can at the state park. Jack wouldn't believe it if he found them in our home. He likes to think of himself as a health freak, and I suppose he is. In some ways, at least.

I check my watch. It's almost 9:00 a.m. I hope Jack isn't running late. I don't want to start today off on the wrong foot. Our reconnection road trip must commence by 10:00 a.m. I would have liked to be on the road already. But he had other plans. I heard his car pull out of the garage before sunrise. I brew a cup of coffee and head upstairs for a shower. I'll be ready at 10:00 a.m., and I know he will be too. As much as he likes to pretend it's not there, we still have it. He'll see.

I'm showered, dressed, packed, and ready to go. Jack is not here yet though. I pick up my phone and call him.

"Where are you? It's 9:20," I say before he can speak.

"I know, I know. Coast Highway is closed, both directions at Cliff Drive, so I'm taking back streets. Have no idea what's going on, but I'll be there as soon as I can. Likely ten more minutes." He sounds genuinely panicked, so that makes me feel better.

"See you then," I say and hang up. I must admit a little piece of me thought he might not come back home after his workout. That he might simply stay at The Club, start his new job, leave me in the lurch.

But he's coming home. I feel my cheeks stretch with a grin and walk to the hallway mirror and check my hair and makeup. Not bad for a forty-something woman. I decide to flip on the news as I wait for Jack. As is typical this time of year, scrolling white letters announcing another fire with another name pop up, this time in Orange County.

This was never something normal, or everyday, when I was growing up. Fires were rare; still scary, but rare. Now, it's like a predictable, ever-expanding season. I'm not a political person, but there's no denying the climate has changed, no denying it at all. The droughts, the fires, the smoke in the air. It's all enough to make you on edge all the time, even if you try not to think about it. During the 2008 fire here, flames reached the house two doors down and destroyed the one three doors down. We were lucky to be spared, we thought. But as we moved back in, we were surrounded by a surreal scene of carnage and charred pieces of people's lives. And smoke, smoldering chemicals, remnants of furnishings and appliances, electronics, and memories. Fire is all-consuming. Jack's parents died in a fire. I shudder at the memory.

"Hey, I'm home," Jack says, finding me in the family room.

I click off the television. "Great! You think we can leave on time? I'm so ready to get out of here!"

"Sure, give me five minutes and we can leave," Jack says. "Any word on what's happening on Coast Highway?"

"Nope. Probably a bad accident. Luckily, we don't need to drive that way. We're headed due east today." I hold up one of the five guidebooks I've purchased. "I'll go punch the destination into your car's navigation so we don't waste a minute."

Jack's face falls. "I didn't have time to get the car cleaned. I meant to. Don't worry about the nav system, I'll just use my phone. I prefer that. Be back down in a minute."

Was he acting weird about me being in the car without him? Yes, he was. I do wish he had taken the time to get it cleaned. Would have been a kind gesture.

We need to be kinder to each other, that's all we need. Oh, and some wild sex. That too.

"Hurry, handsome!" I call up after him. A term of endearment, one from our first dates. I wish we could go back to that time, the innocence, the love. Maybe we will find it again in Utah? It would be nice to find something loving there for a change.

10
THEN

JILL

I'd opened the door, beyond excited, and there he stood. Big man on campus, my steady boyfriend Jack, holding a bouquet of flowers for me. He was picking me up for his fraternity's fall formal, a long weekend starting with a Thursday night event and continuing until Sunday morning, all held in early November at some rich fraternity brother's private lake house in the mountains.

I was a nervous wreck about the whole weekend, but Michelle had helped me pick out what to wear and what to pack. I'd never been to an overnight formal; she had, so that was great. Michelle had me feeling confident and relaxed until the moment I handed Jack my small suitcase. That's when my practiced calm disappeared, to be replaced with a huge anxiety attack. I began shaking all over.

"Hey, Jill, what's wrong? Are you having a seizure or something?" Jack had asked, big brown eyes filled with concern.

"Oh heavens!" Michelle appeared, wrapped an arm around me, and handed me a paper bag. "Breathe into this now."

As I did what she instructed, Michelle introduced herself. Explained that this had only happened a couple of times and attributed it to asthma and the weather change. She'd winked at me.

"Does she carry an inhaler? Are you sure she's ok to go to the mountains?" Jack had asked.

"Yes, she has everything she needs right here." Michelle patted my suitcase. "And here." And touched Jack's arm. Was she flirting? No, she was trying to stall.

Finally, I felt myself calming, relaxing. I hadn't had a panic attack for years. "That came out of nowhere. I'm so sorry." I'd been having a lot of tension because some people were trying to come between Jack and me. I'd gotten myself too worked up. It was a mistake I wouldn't make again. Instead, I'd fix things.

"I'm glad you're ok," Jack said.

"You two have so much fun!" Michelle said, snatching the brown bag from my hand and disappearing into our apartment and slamming the door.

"Shall we?" I asked brightly. I could sense the doubt clouding Jack's vision of me, a vision that had been full of desire. Now it was fused with worry.

I grabbed his face between my hands and pulled him in for a kiss. Sparks flew, for both of us. I trailed my hand down his chest, to the top of his pants. "You're so handsome."

"Yes, let's get going," he said. And just like that, I knew this was the man I was going to marry. That night, during fall formal at the lake, I would solidify everything. I'd make sure of it.

"Sorry again I have to leave a bit early to get back for the LSATs," Jack said as he helped me into his shiny black BMW.

The rest of the weekend attendees would leave on Sunday afternoon, but we'd head back to campus on Saturday night so he could take his LSATs for law school admission on Sunday afternoon. Unfortunate timing, but he had to get a better score or law school would be out of the question. Besides, two nights with all of his fraternity buddies and their dates was plenty of socializing for me.

"No problem. I just want to be with you," I said. "I can help you study too."

Jack smiled, kissed me on the lips, and said, "How did I get so lucky?"

He didn't realize luck had nothing to do with this.

11
NOW

JACK

We've made it through Las Vegas without much traffic besides the LA nightmare, and we are cruising along without much small talk. That Jill can read a book in the car amazes me. I would be carsick by the end of the first page. She's reading all about our first stop, Zion National Park, and the "splendid" old lodge we will be spending the night in.

All I can think about, though, is Erica. She's sensitive, and still hurting from the breakup with her first husband even though he is a complete ass. He dumped her for a pole dancer, she tells me, but at least she got the beach house in the divorce and half of a large bank account. She told me the house was the only physical asset she asked for. Sad thing is, she's never lived here in Laguna Beach, never visited the beach house she now owns. But she loves it. We'll build a great life together by the sea.

After this weekend. I had no choice but to practically abandon her along the side of the road. I had to. To my credit, I dropped her at my favorite hotel, and I know they'll take care of her. Coast Highway was closed, and there was no way to drive her all the way home. My wife was waiting. What a mess. How could I be so unlucky? A car crash closes the only road to my girlfriend's house, while my wife is waiting and watching a very specific departure schedule of my own creation.

I'd pulled into the Surf & Sun Hotel. "I'm so sorry I have to do this. But I need to get home. Now," I'd said, hoping beyond hope Erica would understand.

"So you're going to just leave me here, at this hotel?" she said. Not budging from the car. Not making a move at all.

I hopped out and ran around to her door, pulling it open. "Yes, stay here, have a proper breakfast, or a Bloody Mary, or anything. And have them monitor the road situation. Take a town car home. Bill me. You'll be fine. I'm going to get murdered if I'm not home in time. She'll know I'm lying if I'm late." Beads of sweat ran down the side of my face. I felt like a maniac. I was a maniac. I needed her out of my car. I needed to get home.

I want to control my future. Not the other way around.

"Fine," Erica said finally.

I gave her a big hug and kiss and dashed around to the other side of the car. "I'll be home in just a few days and all of this mess will be over."

"You know what," Erica said. "It better be. Or I'm done."

"Jack!" Jill yells, pulling me into the present in time to see a huge semi swerve into our lane. "You need to pay attention. I'm reading and planning. You are driving. Get it?"

I take a deep inhale. "Don't talk to me like that, Jill. I am not a child."

Jill closes the guidebook and places it on her lap. She removes her sunglasses and stares at me.

"What did you say?"

"I said don't talk to me like that."

"Then don't act this way," she says.

"What way?"

"Distracted. Distant. Disinterested."

"That's it? Can't think of any more adjectives that begin with a D?" I ask. I know I need to calm down but she's making it hard. We need to act like grown-ups and come up with a mutually agreed upon dissolution.

"Dickhead," she says.

"Good one." We are third graders.

"Look, Jack, I just want you to watch the road, focus on driving, so we make it to our first stop safe and sound," Jill says. She's placating me. I hate that.

"I want you to stop treating me like a child," I say again. "I agreed to come on this trip so we could talk to each other, like grown-ups. We do need to talk, Jill, and we both know it."

I can feel the anger before I turn to look at her. My wife, I know her well.

"Nothing changes, do you hear me? Nothing," she says. "We'll just keep getting better together."

I glance in her direction. That's the look that gives me shivers of quiet terror. Pursed lips, huge, shiny eyes, wrinkled brow. Clenched fists.

She haunts me, my wife. She holds me here, in this relationship, in this car, for no reason. Maggie is raised and gone, actually has been since we sent her to boarding school, compliments of my mom. My mom specified in her will that any children we had would attend Sarkus Hill from the age of ten and so it would be for Maggie. My mother insisted, and I know it was to keep Maggie away from Jill.

The relationship between Jill and my mom was strained, like a lot of mothers-in-law and daughters-in-law. I didn't want to send Maggie away, but I knew it was a generous gift and a great leg up for my daughter. We could never afford that type of school without my parents' help. Jill was as happy about the development as I was saddened. Our only child sent away meant more time alone for the two of us.

I take a deep breath. As for Jill and me, we have no reason to hang onto each other aside from our shared secrets. But if we can come to some sort of agreement, we can both move on. I need to help her see this option. But a huge part of me fears she won't ever let go.

"We will keep us. It's comfortable. We are a good team," she says. I've heard the refrain before, more often these last few years.

"Comfortable isn't happy," I say. "We both deserve to be happy again. I think we can come to an understanding, Jilly." I need to find a way to make her listen to reason.

"We will keep us, no matter what. Got it? Love?" Jill says. "My darling."

My wife. Isn't she grand? I grip the steering wheel with both hands and resist the very strong urge to veer off the highway or crash into an underpass.

12
NOW

JILL

The past few hours in the car were miserable. No matter how much I wanted to engage Jack in a discussion about Zion National Park, he pouted. I'd told him about how every single hike in the park would lead to astounding viewpoints of pink, orange, and crimson rock formations. Nothing. No comment. The Zion Lodge is rustic and built in the 1920s. Would you like to know what famous people have stayed there, I asked him. Crickets. Wouldn't even answer a question. So finally, I just let him pout.

We are about an hour out, thank goodness, and have stopped for gas. Jack is inside the tiny hole in the wall, and I'm stretching next to the car. He's been inside for a very long time. The pump has clicked off. The gas tank is full.

I read about this station online and suggested stopping here. The last clean bathrooms before we get to the park. I guess Jack likes my choice since he's standing inside chatting the ear off the man behind the cash register.

The guy's name is Ben. He's my second cousin, or something. Jack doesn't know that though, he just thinks he's a friendly gas station attendant. He is that, but he's also a spy of sorts. I prepped him earlier in the week, and Venmo'd him enough money from my secret savings account that he'd do what I asked, despite the fact he hadn't heard from me, or of me, for two decades. Money speaks louder than all those years apart, I suppose.

Thinking about our money situation stirs up another urge. We need to fix our money problems. It's one of the number one reasons why couples argue and fight, and we are no exception. But unlike most couples, we're creative. We call it having fun, or at least I do. We need to go on a fun little stealing spree soon. Our joint account is dangerously low, although Jack doesn't seem to care. I wonder if he's hiding a secret account from me? No, that's impossible.

I reach down and touch the toes of my hiking boots, just in case Jack can see me from inside the store. If Jack is watching me, I know he'll get turned on. He loves me in shorts, always has. But I'm getting bored. What I want to do is go inside and find out what Ben has discovered about Jack. But I can't. Ben has been instructed to text me everything he learns as soon as we pull out of the station. I hope Ben hasn't decided to become friends with Jack or something.

I wonder if Ben decided to rat me out. A chill rolls down my spine.

I'm going to need to go in there.

I walk around to Jack's side of the car, pull the keys from the center console, and close and lock the door. I'm crossing the parking lot and almost to the front door when Jack walks outside.

The sun is bright, and hot, and I'm squinting but I think I see a smile on my husband's face. He busted me, I know it.

"What are you doing?" he asks. What does that mean? What am I doing coming into the station or what am I doing spying on my husband during a gas station break?

"Nothing," I say with a shrug. "Need to use the bathroom."

"Now?" he asks.

I'm convinced there is something up, but I'm not sure Ben revealed anything.

"Yes. I thought I could wait until we got to the lodge in Zion, but I can't. You took too long."

"Nice guy, the guy in there. He was telling me all about the area. Really knowledgeable about a lot of things," Jack says.

"Uh huh, well, at least you'll listen to someone about Zion. It's going to be extraordinary," I say. I'm trying to convince myself he doesn't know anything. "I'll be back in a minute."

I pull on the glass door covered with stickers, advertisements, and warnings and step inside.

"Can't believe it's really you, Jilly," Ben says. His hair is still the same red, still the same haircut we had as kids.

"Great to see you," I say. "Thanks for helping me."

"Sure, but I've got to say he doesn't seem like he's depressed." Ben shrugs. He has a toothpick sticking out of the side of his mouth and he's talking too loudly.

"You just never know, do you? You didn't say anything about knowing me, right?" I ask once I've reached the counter. "I don't want him to think I'm watching him too closely, you know. That might make him even more depressed. I'm just so worried about him."

"Nah, I said I wouldn't tell him we knew each other, and I didn't. He seems fine, really," Ben says. "You know, a lot of folks back home would love to see you. Maybe family is what he needs?"

I feel a little bad about painting the picture that Jack is depressed, but in a sense he is. He's confused, misguided. He has abused my trust. I focus on Ben.

"Thanks, but that's not what we need. I moved away for a reason," I tell him. "Did you find anything out, anything at all that could help me? He's just so very sad."

"He made two calls. One person didn't answer, and he was angry about it, but he didn't say a name. The other call was to a person named Maggie. He told her he loved her, and he'd see her soon. Is that the mistress?" Ben's eyes widen like he's watching a scary movie. Ben would never cheat on his wife, would never ask someone to spy on his spouse. This is all quite stunning to him, I'm sure.

And not helpful, not at all. I choose to ignore his question. One little Google search would show that Maggie is the former mayor's daughter, but then, Ben isn't the sharpest tool in the shed. That's why I picked him. "Thank you so much, you've been quite helpful. Really good to see you too, Ben. Hope your family is well."

"We're good, Jilly," he says. "Can I tell Uncle Curt and Aunt Sheila I saw you?"

The familiar ping of guilt zips around my heart, but not through it. "I'd rather you not. It will only stir up old hard feelings. My parents made their choice, and I made mine. I've got to run. See you again, sometime."

"Hope so. Be well. And if that guy is as depressed as you say he is, I wouldn't let him go hiking alone. There are some dangerous trails and people have used them to, well, you know."

"I know. I was worried about that the minute he suggested this trip."

"He said you made the plans for the trip, even told him to stop here," Ben says. "He says he'd much rather be at home, at the beach, with this heat."

I feel my face flushing as I hurry out the door. "What can I tell you, Ben? He's a good liar. He has you fooled."

13

THEN

JACK

I fell in love with Jill the moment I spotted her standing on the porch of our frat house. I'd never felt the way I did about any other girl I'd dated. And I dated my share by senior year in college.

She was different. Innocent, but with an edge. And our bodies just fit together. Like it was meant to be between us. And when she finally let me take her to bed, just before the formal weekend, it was fantastic.

By March of my senior year, I knew she was the one, and I had to make it official. Quite honestly, I wouldn't have graduated without her support, her unconditional love.

"What's the rush, son?" my dad asked when I drove to their place in Bel Air to explain my plans one sunny spring Sunday. We sat on lounge chairs by the pool, sipping fresh juice squeezed from oranges my mom picked that morning from their tree. Everything about my childhood was encapsulated in this scene. Sweet, spoiled, perfect.

"No rush, Dad, but you and Mom were high school sweethearts, and you got married during college." My mom joined us on the pool terrace, taking a seat at the table under the forest green umbrella.

"Well, things were different back then," my mom said. She was timeless elegance, pearls and house dresses, dinner parties and fresh flowers. I miss her so much my heart hurts now thinking about her. "You have all the time in the world. If she is the right one, she'll wait. You'll see. Besides, you have law school to worry about. Focus on that, and then the rest of your life will unfold."

"She is the right one. I know you met her during a hard time, and I know that's clouding your judgment. But she's been there for me, helped me so much. I love her. I need her. She reminds me of you, Mom." I was the idiot who believed what I was saying back then.

"Where is she from again?" my mom asked, spinning her gigantic wedding ring around her finger. A favorite habit when mulling things over.

"Bay Area. She is from a wealthy family, the Larkin family, but her parents are deceased. She lived with her aunt," I said. "We'll invite her to the wedding."

"I've never heard of the Larkins from the Bay Area," my mom said. "More orange juice?"

"Mom, don't be a snob. You didn't come from money," I said, walking over to her and kissing her on the cheek before pouring more juice from the crystal pitcher.

"You're right, but it would have been easier if I had, right, dear?" Evie Gardiner Tingley was meant to be rich, even when she wasn't. "And, son, I'm not sure now is the time to draw attention to yourselves, if you know what I mean?"

"I would have fallen for you rich or poor, Evie, my love," my dad answered, cutting the tension between us. "The boy will make his own decisions. There's nothing you can do to stop him, so you may as well get used to the idea."

"We cannot have the wedding and reception here, not now," my mom said. We locked eyes.

"I understand," I said. "Of course not."

"Perhaps at the vineyard?" Dad said.

"Thanks, Dad. You guys will both grow to love Jill. I know it," I said.

"Still on track for law school next fall?" Dad asked.

Dressed in tennis whites for his weekly Sunday match, he could have passed for a man ten years younger than he was. Both of my parents were blessed that way. The old law school question also was a regular occurrence. That I had no desire to follow in the Tingley family footsteps and take over the illustrious firm one day hadn't seemed to bother anyone. My thoughts on the matter were ignored. The plan for our family's oldest sons always was: USC undergrad, UCLA Law School, Tingley & Partners for life.

"I'm taking the LSATs again in a couple of weeks," I said. And I was. I'd done miserably the first time I'd taken them. And I skipped the second chance to take them the Sunday of the fall formal.

"Ooh, Jack, I almost forgot! Stay right there!" Mom to the rescue. She was aware of my miserable score on the LSAT, and she also knew I didn't want to be a lawyer, not at all. Dad and I watched as she hurried into the house, returning a few moments later carrying a garment bag. "I thought it was time for a new suit. You need to dress the part, my budding lawyer."

"Mom, you shouldn't have. I have plenty of suits," I said, unzipping the bag and feeling the lapel of the navy suit.

"It's cashmere. Take care of it," she said, kissing my shoulder.

As it turned out, that was the suit I wore to propose to Jill. I was so in love, so caught up in our relationship, that when my mom handed it to me, that's all I could imagine. My new suit, with a sparkling diamond ring hiding in my pocket and a new life about to unfold. It was almost possible to keep any bad thoughts out of my mind when I focused on Jill and our fabulous future together.

She'd helped me get through the past four months, and without her, I wasn't sure I would have made it. She was my rock, my study partner, my friend, and my lover.

I needed her to become my wife.

14
NOW

JACK

Both hands are tense on the steering wheel, and I keep my eyes on the road. I can feel Jill stare at me, waiting for a reply. She's talking about dinner tonight, which is the last thing on my mind. The silent treatment is the only thing keeping me sane now, so she'll just have to deal with it.

For some reason, Erica won't answer my calls, and the only explanation could be that she's mad at me for dropping her at the hotel. I hope she'll forgive me. I hope she understands. At least I touched base with Maggie.

"I said what do you want to do for dinner tonight? The lodge has ok food, but I found a Yelp reviewed spot in the town of Hurricane, so I'll make a reservation," Jill says. She's taken to answering her own questions, which is fine with me.

It's becoming increasingly clear she will never let go of us, not without an embarrassing fight, and I'm at a loss as to how to even begin a civil conversation on the topic. I know what I've promised Erica, and my daughter, for that matter. My parents, God rest their souls, were worried from the beginning that I was moving too fast. That Jill and I had only been together for a year, and in college.

"Hey, Jack, so you're ok with my plans?" Jill asks, pushing my memories back into the sad box of regrets.

"Whatever you want to do is fine," I answer. Because that is the only answer she'll accept, in truth. I should have realized that from the beginning.

My phone vibrates in my pocket, but I don't dare pull it out in front of Jill. I push the gas a little harder, speed a little more, desperate to get wherever we're going, beyond ready to get out of this car.

"Did you call Maggie from the station?" she asks.

"Yes, why, is that a crime? Calling our daughter?" I sound defensive and I am. I'm also wondering how she knows that.

"Did you two make plans?"

"Plans?" I swallow. She can't know, can she? "No, I was just checking in, saying hi, like a normal father." I don't need to add that she is anything but a normal mother. I believe we all know that by now.

"Saying hi," Jill says. "How lovely. Speaking of lovely, look around you. Welcome to Zion National Park."

We are suddenly engulfed on both sides by canyon walls that must be thousands of feet tall. Bands of different colored stone—in reds, yellows, and browns—swirl across the walls.

Erosion has created a collection of domes and points, almost architectural in nature. It's stunning.

"That's the Court of the Patriarchs. Pull over!" Jill commands and I do. We step outside and walk to the viewpoint. "The three peaks are named Abraham, Isaac, and Jacob. Mount Moroni is the reddish peak blocking Jacob."

"Amazing," I say before I can stop myself. I've never seen anything like this before. The sun is beginning to set, illuminating stone faces that soar above us in bright orange. There's a chill in the air, a huge temperature drop from our gas station stop. I remember the text waiting for me in my pocket, likely, hopefully, from Erica. I fight the urge to pull my phone out. "Let's go to the lodge and check in."

Jill smiles. "I knew you'd love it here. A little vacation is just what we needed, right?"

No, that's not what I need. I don't answer. Instead, I open the car door. "Let's go."

15
NOW

JILL

The Zion Lodge is as promised. Rustic. Like an oversized log cabin with many identical rooms. I can't wait to get out of this cramped room and go into town for a nice dinner.

And wine. I'm wondering now why I didn't bring a few bottles in the car. Old habits, I suppose. When in Utah, pretend you don't drink, alcohol or caffeine. Or dance. Or have fun of any sort. No swearing, only gratitude. Working and praying, hoarding food and water for the end of days. Why did I need to learn how to make so many knots with rope?

I shake my head and remind myself it was my idea to take a road trip to Utah, so I need to knock off the pity party. Sometimes, not often, I do miss them. Especially my mom, and dad, and my oldest sister Frances. But then I remember their anger, their constant disappointment at my "unmanageable ways."

The last straw was the warm summer morning I skipped Sunday school and went skinny-dipping. I'd met my best friend from high school, Steve, for a quick swim in the creek that ran between our homes. Steve's family wasn't part of the Church of Latter-day Saints, didn't understand my misery, but he understood me. Sure, Steve and I were attracted to each other, in that clumsy way a girl like me, who was told sex was a sin until after marriage, and a normal teen boy could be attracted. We'd kissed and splashed and laughed until I remembered the time and climbed out on the bank. I was dripping wet and without a towel, yanking my clothes on in a panic.

"What's wrong?" Steve yelled, swimming to the sandy bank.

"I've got to go. They'll know Sunday school is over. I need to be home, making fudge with beans," I answered. "Yes, that's a thing."

"Ok," he said, laughing. "Like sparkle punch?"

"Yes, stop, I know it's all ridiculous." I'd finished pulling my dress over my head and was wringing the water from my long, blonde hair. "I told you, I'm going to go to college out of state and turn my back on all of this nonsense. I'm not like the rest of my sisters. I'm not going to knit, and quilt, and cook, and have a million babies. I'm not."

Steve climbed from the river and wrapped me in his arms and kissed me.

"Stop, you're wet!" I managed pulling away.

"I'll go with you, anywhere," he said.

It was nice to feel my power over him, but I didn't need someone like Steve. I'd smiled and hurried away from my naked friend and bumped into my youngest brother Jed who had watched the whole scene unfold. He was dressed in a white shirt and church pants. He'd likely administered and passed the sacrament that morning.

"Jill. What have you done?" he said, eyes dark with fury.

"Nothing," I answered, pushing past him and turning toward home. "Stop following me around. It's weird."

"No, you're the weirdo. This will be it. The last straw, you'll see," Jed yelled after me. "Mom and Dad already know. They sent me here to fetch you."

A chill rolled down my spine as I realized I'd messed up one too many times. I'd been caught stealing a few things from the local stores, and there had been that party I'd gone to where I got drunk on one can of beer. My mom always thought I'd come around, conform, since all the rest of the kids were perfect believers. I couldn't. I wouldn't. It's important to be the real you after all, and the real me was nothing like anyone else in my immediate family.

I knew my fate.

The door to our room opens and Jack walks in. His "short walk" lasted close to an hour. I'm sure I don't want to know what he's been up to, but I'll ask anyway.

"Where have you been? Our dinner reservation is now," I say, arms folded across my chest. It occurs to me I sound like my father, judgy and sharp.

"On a walk. Let's go," he says, grabbing the keys from the four-drawer dresser, the only furniture in the room beside the bed. "I'm starving."

We walk through the stunning lobby of the inn, past the restaurant where many fellow lodge guests are dining. But I wanted us to have a different experience.

"Why aren't we eating here?" Jack whines, pointing. "It looks great."

"All booked," I say without stopping. But he does.

"I'm tired of driving. I want to eat and go to sleep." Jack turns and walks toward the restaurant before I can stop him. He's speaking with the hostess and turns to me with a grin. "They have room. Come on."

I look around at the guests in this overlit dining room and sigh. The décor of the Red Rock Grill is a combination of wood and stone, with large windows overlooking the floor of the canyon and the soaring stone walls. Our table is a booth sandwiched between two others; a white tablecloth adds some elegance.

The hostess tosses the menus on the table and departs. Jack slides in on one side, I slip into the opposite. I take note of a young couple the next booth over sitting side by side. We did that too, a long time ago.

The waiter appears, and Jack orders a vodka on the rocks.

"We don't have alcohol, sir," the kid says. "We used to have beer and wine, but now we don't."

"That's ridiculous," Jack says.

"Calm down. It's not his fault. Do you want to go get our reservation in Hurricane?" I smile, pleased with this outcome.

Jack stares at me. "No. I'd rather eat, get this day over with."

How romantic.

16
NOW

JACK

I lie in bed, restless. I can't believe how long this day feels, and it's just the start of the weekend. I don't know if I can make it, but I must. Erica finally called me back while I was walking around the lodge. I'd left four voicemails and three texts, begging her to get in touch. I had become beyond worried. I thought she was ditching me. The real reason was a shock.

"My house, the beach house, it's a total loss," she'd said as soon as I answered.

"What? What happened?" I had just been at her house this morning.

"Fire. Started in the state park next to me," she said, her voice wavering with sorrow. "I can't believe it, I just can't. Two homes next to me are gone too."

"Where are you now? What can I do?" I asked.

"I'm at that hotel where you left me this morning. No one is allowed in yet."

I took a deep breath. My dreams of moving into her beautiful home as soon as I finished this trip were dashed. Fine. We can pivot. "You have insurance, we'll be ok. Do you want me to come home? I will."

"There's nothing you can do here," she'd said. "I'm wiped out. You finish what you've started there, and then we'll make a plan. The fire investigator is coming to meet with me in the morning."

"I'm so sorry, babe," I said. "And I'm so glad you weren't home when it happened."

"Me too," she said, then hung up.

I'd called Maggie next, who answered on the first ring. "Did you hear about the fire?" she asked.

"I just did."

"Crazy. It's across Coast Highway from here."

"I know. Thank goodness the firefighters were on it," I said, still reeling from the news. "Hey, thanks for coming down on such short notice, honey."

"Sure, Dad. I'm just glad you're finally making a plan to get away from her."

I swallowed.

I am going to do this. I am going to get out. For my daughter. For both of us. That's the only reason I involved her in my plan. Maggie wants this as much as I do. Besides, I couldn't involve anyone else. And I know Maggie is safe at home as long as Jill is here with me.

"Yes, it's long past time. Although I'll always love your mom." I read that you need to acknowledge that long-term love is still there, always will be, even when a relationship is ending. It's important to the children of the relationship.

"Uh, whatever, Dad. So I've looked in all the drawers in your bedroom, the kitchen, and the living room. There's nothing. Any ideas?"

"I know. I've searched all those places too, many times over the years. There must be something we're missing. Take your time. You have all weekend," I told her.

"I don't like being here. Gives me the creeps," she said. "I probably won't stay all weekend. I have a lot to do back at school."

"It's your family home, and your mom is here with me," I said. But I understood. Jill's parenting style required Maggie to act perfect, smile, and not make a fuss. Over anything. In return, Jill tolerated our daughter, if she didn't ask for attention or love.

I should have left sooner. Thankfully, my mom saw all this coming and took care of sending Maggie to boarding school and funded her college savings account.

"I'll look again tomorrow. We're going to The Sandpiper," she said.

"Who's we?"

"My friends from college. You didn't think I came down here alone, did you?" she asked. "And no, they don't know about my secret mission."

I swallowed my panic with relief and reminded myself to trust Maggie. She and Erica are all I've got, all I care about. "Have fun. Take an Uber."

"Love you, Dad," she said.

"Love you more," I said, then hung up.

All that was left for me to do was eat a miserable dinner with my wife, who's holding me hostage in a marriage I don't want to be in, and wait for my daughter to find the one thing that will set me free in case my attempted discussions with Jill don't go as planned. Oh, and search the web for information about the fire that destroyed my lover's dream home. Best day ever.

I pull the covers down from my face and glance at my watch. It's 2:00 a.m. Beside me, Jill sleeps peacefully, mouth slightly open. A dark thought pops into my mind. A stronger man might take things into his own hands. I imagine my hands around her neck, squeezing as she fights and wrestles for life until finally giving up, wide-eyed, stunned that I'd stood up to her.

I'm not that desperate. Not yet. I will play her game. Tomorrow I will try to be nice, try to make her realize, in the kindest possible way, that it will be better for both of us to move on. I will talk with her in a loving, compassionate manner. I will convince her that she will be better off without me, but that we will still always be friends. We've shared so much.

I close my eyes, pray for sleep. Instead, my best friend since childhood and my college roommate Ted's face pops into my mind. He wants to talk, as always. I open my eyes and he disappears. Somehow, sometime later, I finally drift off to sleep by imagining Erica's hand in mine.

17
NOW

JILL

I wake up to my husband thrashing in bed, hands in fists punching at the same invisible enemy his feet are kicking.

"Jack, my gosh, wake up!" I leap out of bed for safety's sake and call his name again. He hasn't had a nightmare like this in a long time. He stops kicking and punching and begins to moan.

"Teddy," he says.

"Jack, shhh, it's ok," I say, rubbing his shoulder. "I'm here. Everything is fine."

Jack's eyes blink open. "Where am I?"

"On a romantic trip with your wife," I answer with a smile. Poor guy. So stressed. "Clearly, you needed the vacation."

"I had the nightmare again, didn't I?" He sits up. His hair is wild, like he's been through a storm. And I suppose he has, in his own mind.

"It hasn't happened in a long time, so don't beat yourself up. Usually, these sorts of episodes need a trigger. What's the trigger this time, do you think?"

I haven't done anything to cause it, not this time. I'll admit, there have been a few instances when I've wanted to remind Jack of all we've been through. You know, to help him remember all he had to lose if he were to turn his back on us.

I have a great photo of Ted and Jack, fall of senior year, standing side by side in front of the fraternity house, matching grins on their handsome, perfect faces. Whenever I pull that photo out of the closet and display it with the rest of the photos on the dresser in our bedroom, nightmares are sure to follow. Jack's so sensitive sometimes. I don't even have that photo with me on this trip. Of course, I have other things.

"I have no idea." Jack shakes his head.

At least the color has returned to his face. He climbs out of bed and walks past me without as much as a kiss. Rude. He really does need to work on us. It cannot be one-sided all the time.

While Jack is using the bathroom, I decide to check in on Maggie. I won't call her, no; she was out late at the bars in Laguna Beach, I happen to know. I grab my phone and open the home security app. I find it amusing Jack thinks he can outmaneuver me. Inviting Maggie and her gang of Banana Slug hippie friends to come home and mess up our house while we're gone. He knows I wouldn't allow it, would hate it in fact, so that's why he told her yes. Or is there more to it?

Two of Maggie's friends are asleep on my white living room sofa. I push a button. "Grrrrr."

When Jack opens the bathroom door, I slip my phone into my bathrobe.

"What were you just doing?" he asks. Did I seem suspicious?

"Nothing. How are you feeling? Up for a big hike today?" I ask.

Jack exhales. "Not sure that's a good idea. I'm exhausted. A short hike, and then we hit the road. What's the next stop?"

"The hoodoos of Bryce Canyon." I love the wide-eyed look on his ashen face.

"What are those?"

It appears he has seen enough ghosts for one morning. "Hoodoos are the bright orange and pink, gravity-defying limestone totem poles that are the reason everyone goes there. That and the great air quality and stargazing, as long as it isn't snowing."

"I didn't pack for snow," Jack whines, rummaging in his suitcase.

"I brought a puffer coat for you. And some boots. You'll be fine," I say. "It's only supposed to be a dusting, but we'll see. It's going to be great. And another lodge to stay in tonight."

I watch Jack scan our small room. "Great. Sounds great. Um, Jill?"

"Yes?"

"This isn't working," he says.

"What?"

"Us."

"Yes it is. Get dressed. They serve breakfast downstairs and then we'll go for a short hike, get some steps in." I ignore his head shaking as I close myself inside the bathroom.

We've always had an intense love, a unique and enviable love, since the very first moment we met. And it's only gotten stronger. My understanding was that we were a team, bonded for life, by shared experiences, both good and bad. For better or worse, richer or poorer, all of that. Jack's understanding seems to have shifted lately. As if his vows don't matter anymore. He seems to believe that he can walk away and I'll be fine with it. He seems to think his actions don't have consequences.

Poor Jack. He's misreading the situation. It's a bad habit, one I intend to break this weekend, one way or another.

18

NOW

JACK

I have no idea what triggered the nightmare this time. Perhaps it's being forced to be in a car for so many hours, with Jill, just like the night when it happened.

As usual in my nightmare, Teddy came into my dreams like a friend, we chat and catch up, we're walking together down a long-deserted road, a road that leads to the cabin where the fall formal was held all those years ago.

That's when everything turns dark. The sun sets suddenly. Clouds form overhead. Teddy and I reach the building, and everyone is already there. Jill and her roommate Michelle stand in a corner together, wearing formal gowns and big smiles. Ted's date, Sally, stands next to them, also smiling. We are both swept into the room, into the fun, of drinking and dancing. Until the power goes out. And Ted decides to drive home to his parents, leaving a tearful Sally behind. And I drive back to school because I have LSATs. And Jill comes with me.

"Ready?" Jill says. She's put on hiking boots, long pants, a long-sleeved shirt, a fleece, and a puffer vest. "Oh, I'm not wearing all of this here, just getting ready for Bryce and the hoodoos."

I underpacked, significantly. Somehow, I imagined it was always warm in Utah. I guess I didn't give it much thought. I've been focused on what I wanted to say to Jill to make her understand. I'm going to freeze, but here I am. And it's time to talk.

"Are you feeling better?" she asks, zipping her suitcase.

"Sure," I answer. But I'm off, I know I am. I'm tired, more than usual, my stomach is still messed up, and that nightmare came out of nowhere. I'm not sure what is physically wrong. It could be the stress of this tense situation. I resolve myself to talk to Jill today. To make her understand.

"This little adventure of ours should help you feel better," she says. She stops next to me, standing so close our bodies are almost touching. I take a step back, then realize my mistake.

"Don't do that." Her voice is deep, mean, like a punch.

"What?"

"Step away from me. I'm your wife. Team Tingley as your mom would say." She moves closer. "Even though your mom didn't really want me on the Tingley team."

"Leave my poor mom alone. She's dead," I say, wondering when those nightmares will start again. My mom and dad, their horrible deaths.

"Look, Jack, let's start this day over. Hi! I'm Jill Larkin and I'd love to go on a hike with you, handsome." She smiles and winks at me, extending her hand.

Reflexes kick in again and I return the handshake. My wife and I are shaking hands in our motel room. My brain can't process this. But this is good. I want us to be amicable, reasonable. I force a smile.

"Jack, it's your turn to speak," Jill says, eyes twinkling. "You really are just as handsome as the night you picked me up at the party. You finally noticed me after years of trying to catch your eye."

"I thought you said it was your first time at the fraternity house, that you didn't usually go to those sorts of parties." Not that it matters, not anymore.

"I lied. Ha! I'd had my sights on you since freshman year orientation, but you didn't see me, not until that special night. When you asked me over to your apartment, well, I knew I had you. And I just wouldn't ever let you go."

"Why did you lie about this all these years? I mean, that was our first date, and it was all a setup? You'd been lurking around our parties for years?"

"Yep," Jill says, and I see her as she was then—twenty years old, gorgeous, shy, enchanting. She was different, I thought. Not like any other girl I'd met. I got the different part right.

"What else have you lied about, Jill?"

She grins. "Nothing important. I love you, did from the moment I saw you. Nothing can change that."

People did try to warn me. My parents, even Ted.

I remember Ted pulling me aside, one of the last times we spoke. It was the night before formal, and we were at our apartment.

"You're still taking Jill, right?" he'd asked.

"Of course," I'd answered. "Why?"

"Nothing, but some of us have concerns," Ted said, plopping down on our blue leather couch. "Look, I'm not trying to be judgmental or anything, but I know you're getting some serious feelings for her, and I've never seen you like this."

"You're right," I agreed, taking a seat on the couch next to him. "I really like her. I love her even."

Ted took a deep breath. "The problem is she's not what she seems. Like at parties, for instance, she'll be smiling and friendly if you're by her side, but the minute you leave, she turns to ice."

"What?"

"I'm not kidding. Ask anyone in our group, girls included, well, except Michelle, who seems to have a bond with her. Everyone will tell you she's a bitch: unfriendly, unsmiling, cold, and I think, calculating," Ted said, hands folded together. "Look, I'm sorry, but I wouldn't be a good friend if I didn't say something."

"You're exaggerating. You always do."

"I'm not, dude. I know she looks hot, but inside there's something wrong. Like I said, I think she's cold as ice."

19
NOW

JILL

I never realized being back here would bring back such a flood of memories. I guess it makes sense; I did live in Utah for almost sixteen years. Places hold memories that your mind has buried. Returning, walking on the same path your childhood feet traveled down, well, it's bound to kick up some dirt.

On the trail in front of me, Jack seems to be enjoying the scenery. We're walking next to the Virgin River on the Pa'rus trail. It's not too crowded, but we're certainly not alone. The crimson and orange hues of the canyon and its incredible domes are breathtaking, no matter how many times you've seen them.

I think I told Jack I was a virgin that first night we met oh so long ago. I smile at the memory of my little white lie.

Truth is, I was a virgin when I left Utah, despite my skinny-dipping neighbor's pleas, and my parents' dark suspicions. Thoughts of that Sunday morning come racing into my mind like an avalanche.

I'd walked inside our house, still wet, hair stringy, dress wrinkled and damp. My mom and dad were waiting for me in the kitchen. The house was completely silent, as if ten children didn't live there. As if I didn't.

"Jillian," my dad said. "You have pushed us too far, my daughter."

I dropped my head and said, "Sorry. I just don't like Sunday school. It's so boring."

My mom's face was drawn in anguish, wet with tears. She wasn't able to speak.

"You're going to be sent away. This life is not a fit for you," my dad said. "Your Aunt Beatrice will be taking you in. You can finish high school in Piedmont, and then whatever you choose to do is up to you. But you will never come back here, understand?"

"I'm going away?" I asked, my body shaking uncontrollably. This had been what I wanted, but now that it was happening, I went into some sort of shock.

"You'll leave tomorrow. But know you will always be bonded to this family eternally, just not on earth," my dad said. "Go pack your belongings. Perhaps you will return to your faith one day, my child. If not, you will be banished to the outer darkness."

As I turned away from my parents and ran upstairs to the bedroom I shared with three of my sisters, all I could think was: I need a smoke.

I blink away the memories and walk into Jack, stopped on the trail.

"What's wrong?" I ask.

"I'm just tired. It's beautiful, but if you want me to drive to the next park, we should head back to the car and get on the road," he says.

"Maybe you need some coffee or tea? Caffeine will help." I brought some of my homemade tea bags but had no way to heat water at the lodge.

"Sure, we can stop at Starbucks. Do they have Starbucks here?" Jack asks.

"They didn't back in the day. I mean, caffeine is a sin," I answer without thinking, shaking my head.

"Caffeine is a sin for who? Come on," Jack says.

I take a deep breath. He missed my slipup. "Uh, well, Mormons, the members of the LDS faith. No drinking, no smoking, no sex before marriage."

Jack turns his head, and we lock eyes. "How do you know that? Have you been here before?"

I hate it when I slip up. "Just a guess. I mean, it's pretty remote out here, there are a lot of other places that Starbucks could go."

Jack turns back to the trail. I'm not sure if he believes me this time.

20
NOW

JACK

Jill is lying again. But why? And do I care? Not really.

I should have listened to Ted all those years ago. Or my mom. Instead, I defended her. Stayed with her through tragedy. Married her. Had a baby with her. Created a life with her.

We've reached the SUV parked at the lodge. We'd already loaded our bags and checked out. At this point, we could head home, but Maggie is still there and the last thing she needs is her mother showing up while she's there.

My heart sinks. Poor Erica. I tried to find more information about the fire online, but there were no updates to the news stories from last night. Had we been at Erica's home any later that morning, we could have been trapped. I need to reach out to her as soon as I can get time away from Jill. She's sticking to me like glue.

I suppose, since that first night, she always has. My friends were suddenly her friends. My family, her only family. The only person she added to the group was Michelle, her college roommate. Otherwise, it was all me, my friends, my life.

I'm putting an end to it today, no matter her threats. She can have the house my parents paid for, all her jewelry—some of it actually paid for—and anything else she wants. She just can't have me.

When I turn on the ignition, my SUV comes to life. It has much more pep than I do this morning.

"Let's head out, grab some coffee along the way. Sound good?" Jill coos. She's using her overly cheerful voice, and it's as grating as it is disingenuous.

"I'll agree to head to Bryce Canyon under one condition," I say.

"What's that, handsome?" she asks. I think she winked at me. Good god.

"We leave and drive home tomorrow." I turn to make eye contact, to let her know this is nonnegotiable. "And today we talk. Really talk."

"But I have a hotel, a nice one actually, already picked out for Arches National Park."

"No. Sorry."

"Fine. Drive."

I glance at my wife before backing out of the parking spot. I cannot believe she is backing down, and easily, but maybe, just maybe, today is my lucky day. We will reach an agreement. Everything is going to be just fine. We haven't driven more than a few miles, we haven't even left the park, when she clears her throat.

Dread shoots through me like a lightning bolt, goose bumps springing up as if a cold breeze hit the back of my neck.

"We should talk about your nightmare, why it's back," she says.

"No, I'd rather not. We need to talk about us."

"No, I think it's healthy, my counselor Dr. Kline agrees. You need to talk about your nightmare," she says.

I stare at her. "What have you told your shrink?"

"Counselor," Jill says, tapping her fingernails on the side window. "He's a professional, Jack. I can tell him everything. It's confidential."

"No, not everything is confidential," I say and grip the steering wheel. Jill knows what to say, and when. It's her superpower. She couldn't have told Dr. Kline anything. She wouldn't.

"Dr. Kline says recurring nightmares in adults are caused by depression or anxiety, or PTSD. He says you need to have regular relaxing routines before bedtime, and that you need to talk about it, and rewrite the ending." I glance at her and she's holding a pink notebook.

The notebook. The one Maggie came home to look for. It's here. In the car. I reach for my phone, inside my left pocket. I've practiced turning on the recording app without looking, and I click it on.

I glance over at Jill. She's smiling and rubbing her fingers over the cover of the notebook.

21
THEN

JACK

"Get dressed up tonight, ok?" I said, walking into our cramped kitchen and finding Jill studying. She was finishing my paper for philosophy class. I couldn't believe how much she was helping me, how much I'd grown to depend on her. She was my best friend, and my lover, my confidante, and my future all wrapped into one beautiful blonde package.

She popped up and jumped into my arms. "We're really going out?"

"We are," I said. "But I'm not telling you where we are going. It's a surprise."

We'd driven to Santa Monica, to Ivy by the Shore. I knew Jill had always dreamed of eating there in the floral-drenched dining room, sitting next to celebrities. I'd watched Jill looking around the room at the other diners, trying to pick out who was famous, all night.

"I can't believe we're here, Jack, thank you," she said. She was starstruck, and so appreciative. I wanted, right then, to show her anyplace in the world she'd like to see. I wanted to experience everything together.

"You're welcome. Paris is next," I said, repeating her dream destination and watching her face light up even more.

After dinner, two glasses of champagne arrived.

"Cheers!" I said. "I don't know what I'd do without you."

She clinked my glass and nodded. "Don't worry. You never need to figure that out, Jack Tingley. I'm glad you need me. I love you."

I watched as Jill took a sip of champagne. It took a moment before she noticed the generous engagement ring I'd had the waiter slip into the flute.

"Jack! Oh my gosh!"

"Will you marry me?" I asked and dropped to one knee in front of her.

"Yes!" She wrapped her arms around my neck. "You've made me the happiest girl in the world."

"I'm so happy, Jilly," I said and gave her a big hug. I remember feeling at the time that I'd never have to be alone, that anything bad we'd handle together. But that mostly, everything would be good from that moment forward.

And around us, all the tables, celebrities and not, began to applaud our good fortune.

22
NOW

JILL

O h, poor Jack. I surprised him with my little notebook. All our secrets are here, in my hands. Of course, they're also backed up on the cloud, for safekeeping. I snap a photo of each page as I create it so it will live on forever. A time capsule of our love, synced, forever downloadable. Technology is grand. But I digress.

"So, as my gift to you, would you like to try rewriting the ending?" I ask. I pull out a cute pink pen I purchased just for this trip. Pink with a pink pom-pom at the tip. So cute. So girly. So fun. I reach over and tickle his chin with the pom-pom.

"Stop it," he says. His hands are gripping the steering wheel so tight his knuckles are white.

"So how about it? Let's rewrite the ending," I say.

"I don't know what you mean."

"What I mean is, I could, if you're nice, change some of the story in my book. You know, maybe rewrite some parts."

We're out of the park now and barreling down the scenic Zion–Mount Carmel Highway, not that Jack has noticed. Red and rust-colored rocks stretch for miles. We still need to find some coffee for Jack. But I do think he's more awake now.

"Look, Jill. You know this isn't working. We've been together for a long time, shared some good times, and some terrible ones, but that's the past. Let's move on. Both of us have full lives ahead of us. Why don't you just get rid of your notebook. That would be the gift I need."

"You have Maggie at home looking for this, don't you?" I ask. I can tell I'm right by the way he flinches. "So silly. You think I'd leave this behind? Don't underestimate me, handsome." The good news now is she won't have a reason to stay. Jack will need to call off the search and send her little hippie party back to school.

"Our daughter can come home to visit whenever she'd like," he says.

"Not when I'm not there, not then. I don't like that, and you know it. Anyway, back to our story."

I've opened the second part of the notebook. "Oh, this is our engagement day!" I hold up the journal. My loopy cursive is filled with joy. *I've just come home from the most magical date of my life*, I wrote. *Jack Tingley has asked me to marry him!!!*

With my help, Jack managed to finish out senior year with decent grades. He never did retake the LSAT that year, much to his dad's dismay. Not that we spent much time with his parents after what happened. Jack had invited me home for

Christmas, but Jackson and Evie Tingley treated me like an unwanted, somehow terrifying houseguest. When I'd over-heard their big fight—Jack defending me and his parents telling him they couldn't handle having me there—I couldn't resist standing up for us, of course.

"Mr. and Mrs. Tingley," I'd said, walking into the giant library and standing by Jack's side. "I'm not sure why you hate me, but I can tell you do. None of this is my fault, but I'm the easiest to blame. I see that now. And we'll be going. Jack?"

Jack slipped his hand into mine and nodded. "I'm sorry, Mom, Dad. I wish this didn't have to be like this."

"Wait, Jack, stop," his mom had cried. She sensed this was the end of their close relationship. I was certain of it by the way her piercing blue eyes burned into me.

"He'll be back, Evie," his father said. "Let him make his choice now. He knows he'll need us."

I smiled. All I knew was I was winning, and I'd continue to do so. Mr. Tingley had underestimated me, much like his son.

I'd moved into Jack's new apartment off campus a few weeks after, and we spent most of every day together when we weren't in class. He'd basically dropped out of the fra-ternity. Too many memories of Teddy followed him at the fraternity house. It was a week before graduation, and Jack wanted to celebrate the fact we were, in his words, "getting the hell out of here." I still wasn't sure where we'd end up, or what he would do since law school would have to wait.

I glance at Jack, still death-gripping the steering wheel. "Remember when you asked me to marry you, at The Ivy? That was so special."

"I think I was feeling desperate, actually," Jack says, not looking my way. "I think I was afraid of losing you because I had lost everything else. But what I didn't realize was you were the one who made me feel that way. You cut out my other friends, you alienated my parents, you made me like that."

I can't help but chuckle. "Oh no, buddy. You brought all of that on yourself," I say. "Don't even try that. You know what you did. It all started with you, not me. I saved you then, and I'll try to save you now, I will."

As long as it isn't too late.

23
NOW

———

JACK

Why is she doing this to me? I thought she wanted to reconnect, and instead, she's threatening me. I just want to come to an understanding. A peaceful, grown-up parting of the ways. We both have too much to lose if the other starts talking. We need to be able to walk away.

Jill's phone rings and we both startle. She takes the call. I'm not sure who it could be because Jill doesn't have friends, not in the normal sense of the word. She has acquaintances, mothers of Maggie's friends, or her coworkers at the magazine. And Michelle, her college friend. But she doesn't see her often, at least not that I know of.

"Oh, hello, Michelle," Jill says, overly enthusiastically. "So nice to hear from you. Look, we're in the middle of our

Utah trip, remember? And we're about to lose cell service. What's up?"

Michelle is talking, or at least I think she is, because I can't hear anything. And why would Jill know we're about to lose cell service? Has she done this drive before?

And why am I in this car?

"Oh, yes, he's driving actually. We're in the car together." Jill drops her voice to a whisper. "Still the same, I'm afraid."

I can't help but stare at her. What, exactly, has she told Michelle about us?

She smiles. "Don't worry. I'm watching him every moment. Got to run. Call you when we're back!"

What has she told Michelle about me?

"So, what was that all about?" I ask.

"Nothing, just a friend checking in. Hey, I read about the Thunderbird restaurant, it's a great place to stop. Good coffee too. It's inside a Best Western up ahead," Jill says completely avoiding my questions. Instead, she opens the damn notebook.

"Oh, I love this part. First comes love, then comes marriage, then comes baby in a baby carriage," Jill says in a syrupy voice. "I can't believe I wrote that. Ha! I was so young, so in love."

I can believe it. She was obsessed with becoming pregnant, right away. I tried to tell her it didn't make sense. I still had to study for law school, and I could be arrested at any moment. But it's what she wanted, all she wanted she told me. And so we did become pregnant two months after our wedding.

All the while the police investigation swirled just below the surface of our lives, ready to strip everything happy away. I could hardly think of anything else.

My parents had decided to attend our wedding ceremony, even paid for the reception, hosted on our family's wine estate in Paso Robles. On Jill's side, her Aunt Bea made an appearance. She was the only family member Jill invited, the only one, she said, she had.

"What ever happened to Aunt Bea?" I ask. I hope the phone is recording this conversation. "She never met Maggie, never came to visit after the wedding."

Beside me, Jill bites her lip. "Well, to be honest, her job was done."

"Job?" I ask, almost reluctant to learn the truth. If she was going to tell me the truth for once.

"Aunt Bea's job was to raise me when my parents couldn't. She did. I went off to college and her job was done. It was nice of her to come to the wedding. She always did enjoy a big party. Although I would have preferred if she'd listened to me and worn a shade of purple. Her dress, well, not appropriate," Jill says. "Look, I even write about it here: *What in the world was AB thinking when she picked out an orange dress for my wedding???? I mean ORANGE?? She has enough money and taste to know better. It's almost as if she was sending a message. Whatever it was, I wasn't listening. Nothing could ruin the day I became Mrs. Jack Tingley.*"

"Look, I even taped a Polaroid in here of the horrible dress," Jill says. "I'm so glad I added photos to all of my diary entries. Aren't you, handsome?"

I need to take that notebook. Take it and burn it. She's watching me, so I pivot. I need to ask her how she knows things about this state, like cell phones dropping and the coffee stuff. How does she know? She must have lived here. But she's never told me so.

"I know you don't want to talk about it, but did you grow up out here, in Utah? Seems like you know the area, and not just from reading the tour books." I watch her face closely.

Her smile disappears. I will take that as a small win.

"None of that matters. I rewrote my story when I met you," she says.

Well, at least now I know she's from Utah. I knew she wasn't originally from the Bay Area, and when questioned, she'd just mumble that she moved around a lot when she was young. So now I have something. Not much, but something. I've realized, suddenly with a moment of clarity, that I need to learn as much about Jill as possible. You'd think after more than twenty-one years together, I'd know all there is to know about my wife. I don't know her at all, not really. I married a woman who I thought had saved me, but in reality trapped me. I wonder what love feels like without a constant threat. I think of Erica and hope to find out.

In the meantime, I need to discover *something* about Jill that I can use to escape from her, before she destroys me and the future I'm dreaming about.

24
NOW

———

JILL

"Oh, look, there's the famous Checkerboard Mesa rock formation." I point out the window to a huge rock formation that does look like a checkerboard was carved onto it. Actually, it was formed through erosion from freezes and wind, but it's easy to see what you'd like to see sometimes. "Keep your eyes on the road though, Jack."

He tries to hide a yawn, but I saw it. The man is exhausted. I'll take care of that soon, at lunch.

"Fun fact," I say to keep him engaged. "We will gain more than four thousand feet as we drive to Bryce Canyon. Jack and Jill went up the hill," I sing.

"I wish you wouldn't do that," Jack says. He's such a grump.

"Ok, fine, would you like to turn back to our story?" I hold up the notebook. "There's so much here."

He shakes his head. But he doesn't mean it.

"Dr. Kline says it could help your nightmares, you know, if we go through what happened, create a new ending, a better ending, a story that we will stick to for the rest of our lives. Sound good?" I ask. "Besides, we still have two hours until we reach the lodge. After we deal with the nightmare, we'll move on to when you were an elected official and I was proud of you again."

"You are something," Jack says. "I thought you found a restaurant?" He's whining again. I wish I had brought some tea with us in the car. An oversight.

"It was closed. Opens next month." That's true. I lied about it being open to keep him going. "I'll find someplace else, don't worry."

"Great. I'm going to need to stop someplace, stretch, wake up," he says.

I flip open the notebook, to one of the most important chapters, the one that started everything. Without it, there would be no us, I'm sure of it. I suppose I'm selling myself short. Jack could have fallen fast and stayed with me, even without the tragedy. But my bet is his momma would have found him a sweet little someone with a proper pedigree, a fellow UCLA law student, perhaps, or a fellow Bel Air Country Club member. Who knows?

"It's time," I say. I begin to read from the notebook. The entry was written two days after it happened because I was too in shock to write anything the next day, still shaking from it all.

"No, stop it," he says. "Damnit. Why do you even have that book? You can ruin both of us with what is in there."

"That's funny. I'm innocent."

Suddenly we're flying off the road, bumping down onto the dusty, narrow shoulder, still full speed, careening close to the red canyon walls just feet from the car. I'm screaming.

"Stop! Jack, stop!"

And he does, stomping hard on the brakes, sending my notebook crashing to the floor at my feet as the SUV fishtails to a stop.

Before I can get my wits about me, Jack is out of the car. My car door flies open. "Give me that notebook, Jill. I'm serious."

I yank the handle and pull the door closed, locking the car, Jack on the outside. He stares at me through the car window like a crazy person.

This is not quite the way I pictured our romantic reconnection, I think, as I watch my husband walk away in the side view mirror. We are in the middle of nowhere, with only mountain goats and weird rock formations. I discover he took the keys with him when the car shuts down after several warning beeps. The key signal is out of reach.

Now what is he doing, I wonder. I pick up the notebook, undamaged, and check my phone. I have service. If he doesn't come back here soon, I'll call the cops. That would scare him, I'm certain of it.

25
NOW

JACK

'm so mad I'm seeing double, and all I can do is walk away. Far away. Jill is insane, and she's trying to torture me.

I'm far enough away, around a bend, from where I left Jill and the car. I pull out my phone and see I have a bar. One blessed bar of service.

I call Maggie.

"Dad! Oh my god, I've been trying to get ahold of you, and you haven't picked up."

"Honey, I haven't had service, I'm in the middle of nowhere. I'm sorry, what's wrong?"

"Mom has been spying on us this entire time." She's talking fast, as agitated as me.

"What? Calm down," I say.

"Turns out she has cameras hidden everywhere in the house. I didn't find them until I searched for the notebook. And this morning, she turned on all the lights and the TV in the family room and woke up my two friends sleeping on the couch. What is wrong with her? Did you know about this?" Maggie finally slows down. "Wait, where are you? Is something wrong? You're breathing funny."

I'm just about to talk when I spot Jill walking toward me on the shoulder of the highway. I'm almost out of time. "No, I didn't know about the cameras and I'm really sorry. I shouldn't have asked you to come down. Honey, go back to school with your friends. Mom has the notebook here with us. You'll be safer in Santa Cruz. And listen, as soon as I get home from this trip, I'm filing for a divorce. She won't change my mind, not this time. I hope I can make her see an amicable way forward, but either way, I'm finished." I don't tell my daughter what that could mean for me if Jill doesn't keep our secrets, if she tries to take me down. I've decided I'm going to do this, divorce her, no matter what she threatens.

"Good. Oh, I grabbed everything you wanted and took it to your club," she says. "You know I'll help you however I can. I love you, Dad. Be careful in Utah."

"Don't worry about me, kiddo. Love you more, Maggie moo. I've got to go."

Jill reaches where I'm standing, squinting in the bright midday sun. "So, what are you doing?"

"Getting away from you," I answer. "I mean it, Jill. We're done."

She shakes her head. "Let's get back in the car and drive to the lodge. You need something to eat. You didn't sleep well.

You're disoriented, and you almost killed us running off the road like that."

I thought about it. I did. For a split second, just ending it. Slamming the car into the side of the rock canyon wall. But then I thought about Maggie, and Erica, and the job at The Club, and my friends. I can have a good life again, I know it.

But I cannot have it with Jill.

I ignore her and start the walk back to the car. I want to check in with Erica, but I'll wait until I have better service and more space at the lodge. For a minute, I imagine sprinting back to the car and leaving Jill stranded fading away in my rear view mirror. Would she survive? Likely, and I'd be in trouble for abandonment or something.

Instead, I sit in the driver's seat and wait for her to reach the car. The notebook is nowhere in sight, but I'm sure she has tucked it away somewhere. I've decided she can read whatever she wants to me. I won't stop her. It doesn't change anything. Nothing can.

"Such a gentleman, leaving me along the side of the road. Something bad could have happened to me," Jill says, climbing in and buckling her seat belt. "Maybe that's what you were hoping for, huh?"

"Don't be ridiculous," I say, pulling back onto the highway.

"Were you mad at Ted that night, you know, for sort of ruining the dance?" she asks.

I swallow. "Of course not. I hardly noticed he was fighting with his girlfriend. Back then, I only had eyes for you." Like an idiot, I don't add.

"So, we really did leave early so you could study for the LSATs the next day?"

"Unlike you, I'm not a serial liar. Yes, that was the plan."

She pulls out the notebook. I can't make it stop, can't make her stop. My heart starts pounding and I'm drenched in sweat. She hasn't even said a word.

"Ready?" Jill asks but continues without a reply. "Here's what I wrote: *Yesterday was the worst day of my life, and that's saying a lot. What started out as a date to Jack's formal, well, I can hardly write the words. Jack's best friend is dead.*"

26
THEN

JACK

The November fall formal was in full swing when Jill and I arrived. The partying began on Friday night. It had taken about an hour to get to the house in Lake Arrowhead from campus, and we both were giddy with that intoxicating mixture of pheromones and possibilities for the two nights ahead. Add alcohol and well, let the magic begin.

On Saturday night, the night of the dance, Jill wore a long blue dress that matched her aqua-blue eyes. I wore one of my favorite suits, dark navy. I remember when we walked through the door, a hush fell over the crowd. Sure, the freshmen were in awe of the seniors, and I was class president, like my dad had been before me.

The rest of the girls at the party stared at Jill. She squeezed my hand, unaccustomed to the spotlight.

"What do they all want?" she whispered. "Why are they gawking at us?"

"We're sort of celebrities. You'll get used to it." I pulled her into my arms and dipped her, giving her a kiss and the fraternity a show. Wild applause ensued.

"Stop with the PDA, Tingley!" Ted bellowed from across the room. He swaggered through the crowd like the stud he was. This night, he wore a signature bow tie, maroon and white spotted, with a navy suit like mine. We'd grown up together, Ted and me. We did everything together.

"Hey, man, where's your date?" I asked, scanning the crowd. Beside me, Ted swayed, barely standing up.

"Sally, man, she's awful. We just broke up again, and she is hiding somewhere. You know what? I really don't care," Ted said.

"You're drunk, you don't mean that," I said. It was the alcohol talking.

"Look at all these babes. The freshman class has some hotties," he said.

"They're all here on dates. Don't get into trouble, Teddy. Go find Sally, make up as usual." I wrapped my arm around his shoulder. "Set an example for the lads."

"Whatever, I guess," Ted said and disappeared into the crowd.

"Jack, let's dance," Jill said, pulling me by the hand through the crowd in the living room and making to the backyard of the grand home. A dance floor had been built on the grass; party lights and a DJ completed the scene. The lake sparkled in the distance.

"Let me go get us drinks," I said, pointing to the bar in the corner of the yard. "Be right back."

I left Jill by the dance floor, swaying to the music, and by the time I reappeared, she was surrounded by my fraternity brothers. She did look good that night.

"Hey, what's happening?" I asked. As they realized whose date she was, they scattered.

"Your friends are great," she said. "Now can we dance?"

We did. For what seemed like hours. And then we partied with my friends. I was happy to see Jill get along so effortlessly with the guys, and all their dates. Glad to see her mingling around the party, not having to be glued to my side. By the time I checked my watch, it was almost midnight, and I had to take the LSATs in the afternoon.

I spotted Jill on the opposite side of the backyard and waved. We met in the middle of the party.

"Hey, gorgeous. I know you're having fun, but I have to go," I said. "I'm sorry, but I have to get a good score or my parents will murder me."

"I know. Let's go. I'm happy as long as I'm with you."

We climbed into my BMW and took off into the night. The narrow, winding streets leaving the lakefront were dark, no streetlights, no other cars.

Jill had reached over, touched my thigh, her fingers taunting me.

"Hey, let's wait until we get back," I said.

"Why?" she asked.

I took my eyes off the road for a second, maybe two, and by the time I looked up, there was a person in the road. There was no time to stop, even though I tried to brake. I watched in horror as my best friend's face hit the windshield with such force he cracked it. Ted's body flew over my car and landed behind us on the street

I stopped the car and ran to Ted's side, feeling for a pulse, telling him everything would be ok. I was afraid to move him, afraid I would hurt him more.

"I'm here, buddy, don't worry, we'll get help." I was crying, shaking, inconsolable.

Jill appeared next to me. Bent down, touched Ted's wrist. "He's dead," she said, with calm certainty.

"He can't be, no, it's impossible," I screamed. "Why was he in the road?"

"I don't know, but he's dead, and we need to go." Jill tugged at my sleeve, dragging me away from my best friend.

"We can't leave him here," I yelled at her. "He's like a brother."

"It's all we can do. Your life will be ruined. You'll go to prison, or worse. We need to go now, Jack, before it's too late." Jill pushed me into the passenger seat and ran around to the other side of the car, slipping into the driver's seat.

Before I knew it, we were on our way back to LA, leaving Ted in the middle of the road, like an unfortunate deer. A roadkill.

Even now, after all this time has passed, I still can't believe it happened.

But it did.

27
NOW

JACK

Beside me in the car, Jill is fanning me with the notebook. "You look like you're going to pass out."

I'm dizzy and I can't catch a breath. Outside the car, the street sways. I feel sick, stomach churning.

"I was just remembering the sound, when we hit him. The thud, his face in the windshield, locked in a scream," Jill says, waving the notebook. "Pull over, Jack. I'll drive."

I'll never forget Ted's face either. I see it in my recurrent nightmare. The night that ruined my life.

The night that bonded me to Jill.

And now, I'm driving somewhere in Utah, hyperventilating. The road dips and sways in front of me. I blink my eyes rapidly.

Jill slaps my face. "Pull over now."

I do as she says.

28
NOW

JILL

I had to take charge that night, like now. Jack looks strong on the outside, but inside, he's just not.

We had to leave Ted. What other choice did we have?

Did Jack want to go to prison for killing his best friend? No. Would he want to ruin his reputation for the rest of his life? No. Jack Tingley needed to remain innocent and free, untouched by death and controversy. And I made that possible.

"Breathe in and out," I say as I pull our car back onto the highway, and as an eerie déjà vu of the night I drove us away from the scene settles between us.

Back then, on that dark night, Jack had stared out the window, looking at the crack his friend's face had made in the windshield. Meanwhile, I was attempting to figure out where we would ditch his car. The only place I could think of was his parents' house. They had plenty of space, and privacy. And, I happened to know, Jack's dad drove the same type of car, same color, same everything. It was a perfect solution.

"We need to go to your parents' house. Side streets. Do you know the way?" I asked.

"No, we can't involve them. My dad will kill me," Jack said and started crying again. "This can't be real."

You know how there are two types of people? One type are the folks like Jack who freeze in a crisis. They sit belted into the airplane seat while the other type of people trample over them to escape a fiery crash. Jack would still be on the plane when it exploded. Me? I'd be the first one out.

My plan was to drive Jack to his parents' house, drive through the gates and into their five-car garage. One spot had to be open for him, like always. Next, we'd call a cab and go back to campus. In the morning, we'd come back to Bel Air and explain the situation to his parents. It was Sunday already, and the staff had the day off. In the morning, I would have Jack ask his dad if he could borrow his matching BMW, and we would do a little license plate swap.

But Jack's mom heard something outside, likely the gate opening, and the next thing we knew, the yard was flooded in light.

"Shit, shit, shit," Jack said next to me. "We woke them up. Damnit."

"We were going to need to tell them anyway," I answered, my heart thumping with the prospect. "I'm pulling into the garage. We need this car out of sight."

As soon as we walked out of the garage, we were met by Jack's dad, his gun, and his mom.

"Son, mind telling us what you're up to at two a.m.?" his dad asked, lowering the gun.

Beside me, Jack lost it. "I need, we need, your help." Crying again.

Both of his parents turned to me, like this was all my fault, when it wasn't.

"What happened?" they asked in unison.

"Jack ran over someone on the way home from formal tonight."

Evie gasped and leaned against her husband.

"We need to get inside, now," Jackson commanded, holding his wife with a strong arm. "Son, now."

In my notebook, I taped a photo of the front of the BMW, with the bloody cracked windshield. I always had my Canon with me, always. I snapped a photo of the inside of the Tingleys' garage, and it's in here too. On the next page. Jack doesn't know I have all of this evidence, of course. My security blanket in a diary form.

In my notebook, I wrote: *This is the worst day of our lives. I feel so sorry for Jack, and for Ted, of course. I was beside myself, barely able to follow the conversations between Jack and his parents. But they made a plan, the three of them. A plan to save Jack. His parents would give Jack and me his dad's BMW to drive back to USC, and we would pretend everything was fine. They decided everything and told me I must do what they said. Jack would even take the LSATs that afternoon.*

They really believed everything would work out. I guess for the Tingleys, most of the time, it did.

Jack almost broke the lucky streak, if I hadn't been there to help him. He's so fortunate I love him so much.

"Can you stop talking about this already," Jack says, his voice full of pain. "I can't bear it."

"Oh, Jack, but there's so much more," I say. "Your parents were so mean to me that night. I didn't write that down, but do you remember when they accused me of leaving Ted on the road alive? Like I didn't know how to take a pulse or something? I mean, rude. And remember, your mom wanted to call the police and tell them everything? You would have been ruined, Jack. Ruined."

Jack moans in the passenger seat.

"Well, lucky you. You got away with it all, didn't you, handsome?"

29
NOW

JACK

I look over at Jill, driving along as if nothing has happened, and it reminds me of that night, in the car heading back to LA, after I ran over Ted, killed him, and left him alone in the middle of a dark road somewhere near Lake Arrowhead. Jill was calm, while I fell apart.

I need to pull myself together. Where did she put the notebook? Maybe I can find it now. The light pink cover and the swirly, girly cover title—The Story of Us—belies what is inside her journal. I know that much without ever reading it. I need to pull myself together, pretend I'm trying to reconnect, or I may not survive the weekend. I need to find that notebook to make filing for divorce a safer choice.

"Feeling better?" she asks. "We're about twenty minutes out. We'll eat. Recharge the old batteries."

"Sure, ok," I manage. I'm scanning the car, but she catches me.

"You won't find it, Jack, so stop looking. We're almost through that part, anyway, do you want to rewrite the nightmare?"

The second most crushing image of my recurring nightmare is the one I didn't witness, but only read about in the news. The one where the restaurant supply semitruck runs over Ted's body an hour later. Like me, the truck driver didn't see Ted until it was too late. Unlike me, the truck driver called the police and stayed at the scene.

My stomach turns. "There is nothing to rewrite. What happened, happened. And you're almost as guilty as I am," I say. "You told me to leave, you drove us away from the scene."

"Oh, handsome, as you well know, the statute of limitations is waaay over for that crime now. Remember all those years of living in fear. That nasty investigator trying to prove we were involved, you were involved. Ted's parents sniffing around. Horrible," she says. "So let's pretend Ted lived. He wasn't on that road that night. He was making out with Sally at the party. Let's pretend you did great on your LSATs and got into UCLA Law School as per the family plan."

My shoulders relax at the fairy tale. My life, the way it should have been, could have been. The life I didn't want until I couldn't have it anymore.

"Ok, so, it's not real," I say. I spot the notebook. It's on the floor at her feet. No way I can grab it without causing a crash. Maybe I should? Unfortunately, I know there are more incriminating stories in it, ones that remain chargeable. I need to get that notebook.

"Would we have been together if Ted hadn't died?" she asks. "I mean, your mom never liked me, your dad tolerated me, and you were known to be a ladies' man. You had so many options, such a big future."

I'm not going to answer that question. The honest answer is I really liked Jill, but if things had been different, I would have moved on; that was just the way I was wired back then. But I can't be honest with her. I need to keep her calm to try to get the notebook. She doesn't deserve the truth. She doesn't deserve anything. This was all her fault. I should have stayed with my friend, waited for help to arrive, driven him to a hospital. Something, anything other than what I did.

What we did.

"Of course we would have been together, honey. We were meant to be, don't you think?" I smile and touch her thigh.

She looks as if someone has spooked her. Eyes wide, head tilted in wonder. "That's the nicest thing you've said to me in a long time. The last time you told me we were meant to be was when I held the Bible so you could be sworn in as mayor. Those photos show such a happy couple."

That was a great moment, I realize. I loved being a politician. And I suppose we were happy for years; stuck together, but happy. But when Maggie left for boarding school, I started to see Jill more clearly. I started to want to escape. Our secrets had eroded our relationship, both the ones inside and out. And we're beyond fixing. At least in my eyes. Because now I've discovered what real love feels like. And it's much different than this. I've been in denial for too long.

"That was a happy time," I answer. "We had some great times, Jill."

"And so many more to go," she says.

Outside the window, the landscape has changed dramatically. "Wow," I say because I can't help it. "Look at that. Miles and miles of what look like weathered totem poles."

Jill pulls off into a viewing area, and we sit in silence looking at the scene. "Bryce isn't really a canyon. It's an amphitheater in geological terms. All those hoodoos are made of rock. The top rock is called the cap stone, and it's harder than the layers below. Hoodoos are permanent, even as Bryce continues to erode. Old hoodoos die, but new ones are constantly forming as the amphitheater rim recedes. Lovely, right?"

I pretend I'm caught up in the moment and kiss Jill on the cheek. She's as shocked as I want her to be.

"Thank you for bringing me here. It's stunning," I say.

"Well, of course, handsome. Let's go eat and then we'll explore," she says.

I force a smile and squint so it reaches my eyes. My lovely wife believes it's real, and that's a relief. I've realized I can't fight fire with fire.

I need to play a much more subtle game. And I will. From now on. She's opened the deepest wound, the event I avoid thinking about, the one thing in my life that haunts my sleep. She's provoked me with our past. I need to stay focused on my future, one without her in it.

30
NOW

JILL

Of course, I've done my research, and not just on the national parks of Utah, and not just about which one of my distant cousins may come in handy during this trip. No, much more. For example, the statute of limitations for a felony hit and run is six years after the accident scene is discovered. In our case, it was the same night. We only had six years to worry, I'd told myself and Jack numerous times.

But then again, I wasn't one to worry. Like I said, I'm a person of action.

I pull into the Bryce Canyon Lodge parking lot and find a spot close to the entrance. There aren't many other tourists here now, and I hope it stays that way. I also hope Jack's little lovey-dovey moment was for real. I mean, you should have seen us when we were younger. Couldn't keep our hands off each other, after the accident, as we call it still.

The funeral was tough though. Even for me. Looking at Ted's sister, and parents, and even Sally sobbing out of control and knowing my boyfriend was responsible. Well, that wasn't easy. I think about opening that page in the notebook, but Jack's already out of the car, has popped the trunk, and is unloading the suitcases.

Maybe later, tonight after dinner, we'll revisit some more memories. It seems to be making him feel better after all. He's calmer, nicer even. Maybe Dr. Kline was right. I shake my head. Dr. Kline can't be right because he doesn't really know anything about me, or Jack, just that he thinks Jack is suicidal because I told him so. He doesn't know about Ted, or anything else. I know Jack thinks I've told him everything, but that would be stupid and careless. I'm careful and smart. Very smart.

"Hey, can you roll your suitcase? I have everything else, honey," Jack says.

The use of these terms of endearment is killing me. Honey? Really? He could have started by just being nice. But I suppose this change of heart is something I should embrace. Who knew retraumatizing someone, dredging up one of the worst things that happened to them, and sharing that experience, would bring us closer? Well, I guess I have reminded him of how much I did for him. How much we've been through together.

"Coming, dear!" I say, trying out a new endearment, grabbing my notebook and heading to the trunk.

As I round the corner, I think I see a strange look in Jack's eye. Wary, plotting. No, I tell myself. He's come around to our future. All's well. Or at least it better be.

"You should grab those coats too, Jack. It's really cold here at night, handsome." I toss mine back at him with a smile.

"Got it. Thanks again for bringing them," he says, slamming the trunk.

We begin our trek to the lodge in silence. It's much like the one in Zion National Park, built in the 1920s, log cabin style. The famous lodge in Yosemite was built by the same architect with a goal of bringing nature to people with large windows, great settings, easy access. I'm dying to sit in one of the oversized Adirondack chairs on the porch.

We push in through the rustic doors and step into a reception area with huge stone fireplaces on each end and a smiling receptionist behind the front desk.

My cousin Rhonda. What the hell is she doing here? She looks exactly the same as I remember her: gray hair, pulled into a tight bun, reader glasses on a chain around her neck. But I have changed. I'm all grown up now. I must believe she won't recognize me, although I wouldn't be surprised if Ben tipped her off, the traitor. Each time I called the front desk to plan our trip, the phone was never answered by a person named Rhonda. I'd searched the staff comments and photos of every place I booked to make sure I didn't run into anyone I didn't plan to see; none of my family was listed as working here. But this is fine. If she recognizes me, I'll deal with it.

"Welcome to the Lodge at Bryce Canyon," she says with a smile, a clueless-that-I'm-her-cousin smile.

"Thanks so much. Happy to be here," I answer.

Jack says, "I'm starving. Are you serving lunch, please, I beg you?"

"He's a bit dramatic, but we are hungry," I say and punch him softly on the arm. He wraps his arm around my waist!

"Yes, you are in luck. We just started serving all three meals again. During the summer, it was only dinner because there are so many other options around here. Not so much now. Just leave your things and go right over there to the dining room. Can I have the name on the reservation? I'll check you in and store your luggage," Rhonda says.

Helpful, my cousin. Clearly, thankfully, she doesn't recognize me.

"Jack and Jill Tingley," Jack says.

"That's so cute. Like the nursery rhyme?" Rhonda says.

I look at Jack. He's not grimacing but smiling. Wow.

"Just like that," he says with a chuckle.

31
NOW

JACK

As soon as we're seated for lunch, in a dining room that looks a lot like the one at Zion Lodge—beams, huge Craftsman-style lighting, floor-to-ceiling windows framing the view, chunky wood tables with red and white checkered tablecloths—I excuse myself.

I must get phone service. I checked while we were registering, and a faint signal was available near the front desk.

"Hurry back! Should I order for you?" Jill asks as I'm leaving.

"Ah, sure, yes, great," I answer, trying to smile. Light and breezy, that's me.

I dart past the front desk. The older woman—Rhonda, I think—pops her head up. "Mr. Tingley, can I help you?"

"Yes, uh, the restrooms? And where can I get phone service?"

She laughs and my heart sinks. "Well, your best bet is here in the main lodge. Not the dining room though. Sometimes it works down the hall, on the way to the restrooms or by the gift shop. None of the guest rooms have it. Good luck!"

I back away from the front desk and head to a corner by the stone fireplace. No service. I slip outside the door where we arrived, nothing. Back inside, I start down the hallway to the restrooms and bingo, two bars appear on my phone.

Erica answers on the first ring. "Where are you? I've been trying to call, but I get a weird error message. Have you listened to my voicemails?"

"No, I'm sorry, I've been trapped in the car with Jill, and no service. What's happening? Are you ok?" I glance behind me down the hall to be sure I'm not being followed. I have to beware of my own spouse. I've been such a fool.

"They are investigating the fire. They think the fire was set. Arson. They think my house was the target," Erica says, and I can tell she's crying again.

A chill rolls down my spine. Immediately my thoughts jump to Jill. No, it couldn't be Jill. She doesn't even know about Erica. And she was at home, waiting for me. It wasn't Jill.

"I'm so sorry, but I'm sure there is some sort of mistake. I'm sure it was just a careless camper. Who would want to hurt you? This can't be right."

"Well, they have their best investigators on it from the fire department, and of course, my insurance company. They haven't found the source yet, but something about how fast it started and how hot it burned makes them suspicious." She pauses, her voice quivering. "I'm scared."

That makes two of us. "Do you think your ex-husband has anything to do with it? I mean, he didn't want you to get that house, right?"

"I don't know, I guess he's a suspect. They're questioning him. Can you come home? I need you."

I take a deep breath. "Yes, I'll be home tomorrow. Don't worry, you're safe now, just stay at the hotel, and I'll be there by late afternoon, early evening. I love you."

"Ok," she says. "I love you too."

I feel a tap on my shoulder and turn around. It's Jill.

"Lunch is on the table," she says. Her arms are folded across her chest, ice eyes flashing.

"Thanks so much," I say to Jill. Into the phone I say, "Bye!"

I lean forward and kiss Jill on the cheek before starting down the hall. "I'm famished. Thanks for handling. What are we having?"

Behind me, Jill says, "Oh, you'll see. Who were you talking to?"

"Oh, that was Maggie. She and her crew are safely back at school," I say, my heart pounding in my chest. We both wave to Rhonda as we pass the front desk.

Are we the only guests, still? Weird. No one else is in the dining room.

"This looks good," I tell her as we reach our table. I'm having grilled cheese and tomato soup. My stomach growls with hunger.

"I also ordered you some coffee, with cream, you know, to keep you awake. We have a fun hike this afternoon." I notice

Jill only ordered a small salad for herself. She rips off a piece of bread from the basket. She fiddles with something at her neck and pulls the necklace from its hiding place.

"You brought that, here?" I ask. "Seems rather out of place."

"Like me at your parents' anniversary gala," she says. "What an evening."

I stir the soup, taking a bite and trying to remind myself I'm supposed to be playing nice. I'm supposed to be drilling her for information that will help me with the divorce. I take a bite of the sandwich, and gooey cheese spills out down my chin. I look up and she laughs. That's better.

"I still can't believe you did it. And Mrs. Anderson never suspected you," I say.

I remember the evening. Maggie was two, at home with a sitter, and we'd driven up to Bel Air Country Club to celebrate my parents' thirtieth wedding anniversary with all their friends. Jill and I were the youngest in the room by decades. We were seated at a table next to the Andersons, one of Dad's law partners. Dick Anderson kept questioning me about law school, about when I was joining the firm. Mrs. Anderson grilled Jill on her background. It was awkward, uncomfortable.

"She was so sick, poor old woman," Jill says, taking a bite of her salad.

"It was so sudden," I say.

I remember Mrs. Anderson had barely finished half her salad when she stood, clutched her stomach, and looked as though she'd drop dead. Jill sprung into action, rushing her out of the room and away from social embarrassment. She stayed with Mrs. Anderson in the restroom of The Club until the worst had passed, Jill told me at the time. She rejoined our table and told a worried Mr. Anderson he should escort his wife home. After he left, Jill took his seat next to me and gave my arm a big squeeze. That's the moment she slipped the necklace, Mrs. Anderson's diamond and sapphire necklace, into my suit pocket.

"Food poisoning can hit you like a punch. If that's what it was." Jill smiles.

"What was it, exactly?" I ask, knowing she'll never tell me.

"It was a well-executed sleight of hand, resulting in this treasure." She touches the necklace. "Our first time."

Jill told me later, once we'd driven back home to Laguna Beach, that she'd slipped open the clasp as the old woman retched over the toilet. For all she knew, it was flushed away. With the embarrassment of the scene she'd made at The Club, Mrs. Anderson never reported the necklace missing. Poor woman.

"You never forget your first time," I say. I take a bite of my grilled cheese. But when I see her face cloud over, I realize we're on to another topic. I hope it's not another bad memory.

"There's more where that came from," she says. "I have been researching some possibilities. So fun."

"No need for any of that. I have a job prospect now. Everything's fine," I say.

She slips the necklace under her hiking shirt, tucking it away. "We'll find you an appropriate position. Just give me some time to work on it. I have connections, you know, through the magazine."

"We're running out of time, Jill. We've plowed through my inheritance from my parents over the last twenty years, living beyond my salary, way beyond our means. So, unless you've buried a pot of gold somewhere in Bryce Canyon, I need a job." I take another bite of my sandwich and try to keep my tone in check.

"No pot of gold here, I'm afraid. But remember, I do know how to earn some extra cash when we need it."

My heart skips a beat. I reach for my coffee and take a big swallow as my head spins. She can't. Not again. "No, Jill. You promised."

Jill smiles. "Desperate times call for desperate measures, they say. Besides, it's fun."

32
NOW

JILL

Poor Jack. He hates it when I steal things. Some sort of moral compass nonsense he says he inherited from his parents.

I guess if you didn't grow up perfecting your petty theft schemes, like I did, it could be a bit stressful.

Across the table, wide-eyed, Jack says, "No."

"Calm down. There's nothing to take around here. I'll wait until we're home. Drink your coffee. Finish your lunch."

He seems to relax a bit. He's even trying to be nice. I guess he doesn't realize I heard what he said on the phone. Before he lied about talking to Maggie. This will be fun.

"You know, on the other hand, if you do take that job at The Club, it will provide you with a master key, right? Think of all I can find in the ladies locker room," I say. "Remember?"

Jack's face falls at the memory.

It was all about spring break, Maggie's senior year at boarding school. *Everyone* in her class was going to Paris for the week. Maggie was invited to go with a friend of hers, with their family, all expenses paid, but I wasn't about to let that happen. I wanted to go to Paris, mais oui.

Jack put his foot down. "We're running out of money," he said. We sat in our kitchen, talking quietly because Maggie was home for the weekend.

"We would have so much fun. It's her last trip of high school. You and me, the Eiffel Tower, so romantic."

"No, we don't have the money. Right now, I'm trying to figure out how to pay for her plane ticket. The Russells are covering everything else. So nice. Thank god my parents made a college fund for Maggie."

"We're going to Paris," I said. "I'll find the money."

Most of the women around here had too much of everything, anyway. Most of them wouldn't even notice a little bauble or two disappearing, wouldn't bat an eye over, say, a ruby cocktail ring or a third diamond tennis bracelet. These things go missing, they slip off while playing tennis, for example. Happens every day, especially when I'm around.

"I'm going to sell some jewelry," I said. Enough time had passed. The last time I'd done a locker sweep at The Club was three years earlier. I had a fun time at Michelle's country club too, a year before. I'd pawn the items in LA. Easy. "Book tickets for all three of us. Business class. And Jack?"

"What?" He shook his head and looked away. He knew about my habit, and he knew better than to try to stop me.

"Upgrade our hotel room to a suite. This is going to be epic."

"This is going to cost a lot, likely sixty thousand."

"No problem," I answered. "I'll have it by the end of the week, mon cheri."

The trip had been fabulous, although Jack and I didn't have any sort of a romantic time. We followed Maggie and her friends around, drank wine, and stayed up too late in the hotel lobby bar with the rest of the chaperones. But at least we went.

And now I will need money again. No problem. Challenge accepted.

I stare at Jack, his eyes a little glassy. I smile. "You worry too much, handsome. Ready to go for that hike?"

"I guess. I'm still a little tired, but maybe some exercise will help," he says, standing. "I'm looking forward to seeing the sights."

He pulls my chair out for me. What a gentleman. "You're so cute when you're being strong."

I want to believe he's softening, that he's coming back around to us. But he said *I love you* to her over the phone. I heard him. I don't think it was Maggie, despite what he said.

Jack reaches for my hand, and I hold it, all the while fuming. I still can't believe how far this has gone.

33
NOW

JACK

As I follow Jill out the doors of the lodge and into the bright sunshine, I'm hit with a wave of dizziness. I grab at the closest thing, a wooden chair, and fall into it.

"Jack! Are you alright?" Jill runs to my side, rubbing my shoulder. "Talk to me. What is it?"

I want to say *you are the problem, Jill.* My wife is a thief, a liar, a bad mother, and a worse partner. I need to get that notebook, filled I'm certain with things to incriminate me, but more that would incriminate her. Did she write about her jewelry heists? She must have. I can only hope.

"I'm feeling better. Just got a wave of dizziness," I say and stand with her help. We start walking along a narrow path through the woods. Signs point the way to the rim and the hoodoos beyond.

We walk a few minutes in silence, and it's beautiful and I begin to relax, allow myself to imagine coming here again, with Erica, how different that will be. But I need to focus, and I need to get more information about my lovely wife.

"So tell me a little more about your childhood, will you? It would help me get to know you better, don't you think, a way to reconnect?" I say, hoping to be subtle. I've turned on the recording app again, like I did in the car.

"What do you want to know?"

Ok, good so far. "Well, I mean, let's see. Did you, you know, steal stuff growing up?" I ask. I hope my tone makes her realize I'm just curious, having a conversation.

"Yes, I guess, I mean, I always got a rush from it. Still do."

"Do you write about it, you know, in your notebook?"

She stops, turns around, stares at me. Then smiles. "No, that would be stupid. What if it ended up in the wrong hands? I curate my content. Carefully."

She turns and starts walking again.

"So, let me get this straight, you wrote about what happened to Ted, which could have been bad for me if your notebook had ended up in the wrong hands, especially within the first six years after it happened. But not about any of your darkest secrets."

"It's my notebook, Jack. Besides, I kept it safe, you were never really a suspect. But you could have been if they found that BMW, and it seems like they were getting pretty close to finding it back then," she says. "Oh look, we're here."

I knew it all along, I suppose. She wrote her side of the story in her notebook so she would have leverage over me, have some sort of written proof framing me. But even though she has confirmed my worst fears, I'm not changing my plans for a divorce. And I will still attempt to destroy the notebook.

We reach a paved path and the edge of the canyon. Below us, brightly colored hoodoos stretch as far as the eye can see. It's a magical site, and my dizziness returns. I reach for the railing. I remind myself to breathe. Tomorrow, we drive home. Tomorrow night, I'll be with Erica, in her hotel room, and we'll make our plans. I will do anything and everything to protect Erica and our future together.

Erica and I can move to a community close to The Club. I will take the manager's position, and I will see to it that I remain the only Tingley member after the divorce. Jill will not be welcome at The Club. Erica will take her locker in the ladies locker room. Everyone's possessions will be safe from Jill. I will be a hero of sorts, but no one will know. Still, I'll have to watch my back, forever. That's why I need as much on Jill as she has on me. That's why I've been recording her words, her thoughts, her part in our secret life of crime together.

And Jill? Who knows what she'll do when I leave? Even if she showed the notebook to a detective now, there wouldn't be a case brought against me, I'm almost sure of it. But she won't. I have enough on her too, not in writing, but in memory. Thanks to the recordings I've made for the last couple of weeks, and especially during this road trip. So now, we both have the marital communication privilege, I'll explain to her. You keep quiet about my deeds, and I'll keep quiet about yours. There are two broad types of privilege in marriage according to my law school textbooks: the adverse testimony privilege and the marital communication privilege. We have immunity to not testify against each other, and we don't have to share written communications.

The only slight problem is the crime-fraud exception, I've come to realize. When one spouse commits a crime and the other spouse actively participates in the fruits of the crime—like a first-class trip to Paris, for example—or covers up the crime, both spouses become partners in crime and statements made can be used against the other.

Maybe she'll let me go? I stare out at the vast canyon of hoodoos and remember what my friend Doug, the best divorce attorney in Orange County, told me recently while we were golfing. He was speaking hypothetically, but I listened closely. "When one spouse is willing to testify against the other in a criminal proceeding, whatever their motivation, their relationship is most certainly a mess, and there is little in the way of marital harmony for the privilege to preserve."

I am left with two choices. Continue to fake marital harmony to save us both from prosecution, resign myself to life with Jill to protect the world from her. This is the choice I have been making, but since I met Erica, it's no longer enough. I've seen what happiness can be, and I have hope again. To leave, I must get Jill to agree to stay silent, for the two of us to agree to protect our secrets, for the past, for our daughter.

Because there is enough to put both of us away, as I'm sure she knows. But she has all the proof against me in her notebook. I need to get some of my own if I'm to have any leverage in this deal. I need proof against her. And I'm gathering it. If she still decides to give the police her notebook, well, I'll just have to convince them that she is a liar. She is a professional liar.

Jill wraps her arm around my waist, and we appear to be the image of the perfect couple. Anyone watching us would see two people deeply in love.

"There's a three-mile loop that will take us through all of this, all the way down to the amphitheater floor, and back through the Queen's Garden," Jill says. "Think you're up for it?"

Am I up to outsmarting Jill? I hope so. That's why I'm going to play every angle at this point. I will remind her our time together can never be erased, but that things change. I will paint a rosy picture for her, one that includes a new love in her life. She won't be stuck with grumpy old me anymore. Maybe, if I explain it right, she'll let me go. No threats, no strings attached. Just the protection of marital privilege keeping both of us safe as we move on. She doesn't want to stay married to a man who doesn't want to stay married to her anymore, of course not. No one would want that.

Everything is going to be fine. I remind myself I need to pay Doug's retainer, conflict him out in case things get ugly with Jill. Who am I kidding: Things will get ugly with Jill.

I pat her hand, the one wrapped around me. "Sure, I can handle anything with you."

34
NOW

JILL

That's what you think, Jack, I don't say. "Anyway, let's get going."

As we descend the trail, Jack behind me, it feels as if I'm being swallowed up by the earth. The hoodoos begin to loom above us, eerie and crumbling like pink and orange and red sandcastles. The park is strangely empty, and we have yet to see another group on the trail. But I hear them, somewhere below us. I haven't seen a park ranger yet either, but I know they are around, watching us.

Like Rhonda. She's watching us, but I don't know why. I may be being paranoid. But she does seem to be paying a lot of attention to us at the lodge. Does she in fact recognize me from childhood, me, one of a million blonde-haired, blue-eyed LDS girls who visited Bryce Canyon with her family. Or from one of those gigantic family summer picnics. No, not possible. And then I think about Ben, about how he wasn't very helpful, about how Jack told him where we were going.

I'll need to have a chat with Rhonda, explain our situation, poison her view of Jack like I tried to do with Ben and Dr. Kline. I'll tell her Jack is depressed, suicidal even. I'll do that when we get back from the hike. While I'm busy with Rhonda, Jack will have ample time to check in on the person he loves. I feel like screaming. The anger fires inside me, a hot rage I'm working hard to control. It isn't easy, but so far, I've done it. So far.

"Which way do you want to go?" I ask as we come to a fork in the trail.

"The shortest. We have to climb all the way back up there at some point," Jack says, pointing to the rim now high above us.

"That's this way," I say, starting again.

"How many times have you been here, honey?"

Nice endearment placement. Almost sounded natural. Almost. "Oh, I don't know. Would you believe me if I said more than ten times?"

"Even though you said you'd never been to Utah when we were planning this trip," he says.

"You really can't believe everything everyone tells you, handsome." I don't turn around to see his face.

"So, you grew up in Utah, I'm guessing Salt Lake City. I'm also guessing your family was Mormon?"

This is fun. "We don't like that term. It's LDS, the church," I say.

"And Mom and Dad didn't like having a daughter who steals," he says. "Wow, look at that one." He points to an especially imposing hoodoo with what almost looks to be a monster-like face.

"No, they didn't. They also didn't like me smoking, and they certainly didn't enjoy my boyfriend. So, I went to live with Aunt Bea. End of boring story." I stop on the trail, shaded by a very tall, shockingly thin hoodoo. Jack almost bumps into me. We look at each other. "The past is best left there. Understand?"

"Sure, it's just that you knew my parents, know all about my upbringing, and I didn't know anything about yours. You told me your parents were dead. It's a surprising development. That's all, honey."

Is that all? I wonder. Perhaps I should give him another little tidbit from the notebook, another little something for him to think about while we hike. Yes, that would be nice. I reach into my backpack and offer him a water. He takes it, and while he's chugging, I pull out the notebook.

"Why now?" he asks, wiping the water from his face with the back of his hand. "I've had enough of that for one trip. In fact, I think it needs to go." He lurches forward and tries to grab it, but I'm too quick.

"Not so fast, handsome. We're rewriting your ending, remember? Getting rid of your nightmares. Like this, this part, it was stressful. You know all those years between the accident and the six-year mark. I'm so glad we didn't have the wedding at your parents' house. That would have been awkward."

"Awkward? It's what my mom always dreamed of for me, but then, of course, I ruined that too, by involving them. We should never have driven to my parents' house that night," Jack says.

I'm so frustrated by him. "Where else were we supposed to go? We had to get rid of the car."

I remember it like yesterday, driving Jack's dented BMW into the garage, pulling the old tarp over it, leaving it, like a smoking gun hiding in the Tingleys' compound. I open the notebook and turn to the section I called *Fun With Detectives*.

"I'm so sweet, so in love. Look what I wrote: *I hope Jack loves me as much as I love him. I hope the news I'll tell him tonight about the baby makes him love me even more. And I hope he kept his mouth shut and let his lawyer do the talking today at the station.*"

Jack's face turns pale. "You think this is all, what, entertaining?"

"No, of course not. My notebook is The Story of Us, and it's a way to process things. Dr. Kline says it's very healthy." I smile. I start to read. "*UPDATE!! Jack says everything went fine at the station, but he doesn't look good. He has dark circles around his eyes, and the nightmares come every night. The detectives say they have a lead, a new witness. Jack says he doesn't believe them, but his parents are worried and want to move the car. The lawyer says it's too risky to move it. I want to celebrate the baby news, but Jack is too tired. He's always too tired these days. I think the stress of possibly being busted and going to prison for a very long time is really draining. I'll come up with something to help him. I will. I'm his wife, and anything that endangers our marriage is a problem for both of us to solve. If Jack can't, I will. That's what love means.*"

I stop reading and stare into Jack's eyes. "Everything I do is for you. You know that, right?"

Jack sighs. "I know you believe that."

I open the notebook and read. "*UPDATE! I fixed everything!!*"

35
NOW

———

JACK

When she reads from her notebook, her voice changes. It's higher, almost childlike. I don't know what I'm dealing with here exactly, or how she thinks she helped me with what happened, but I don't think she's lying, not now.

I watch her slip the notebook back into the pocket of her backpack. I remind myself of its latest hiding place in case the opportunity arises.

"Honey, what do you mean you fixed everything?" I keep my voice friendly too and reach for her hand. I'm comforted by the knowledge I'm recording her every word.

"You're so thick sometimes," she says. "Handsome."

"Can you read me the part about how you fixed everything?"

"I told you, I don't write that stuff down. Come on. We're late to see the queen."

What is she talking about now? Jill trots down the trail fast, her blonde ponytail swinging back and forth in front of me. I lose sight of her. She's disappeared. I come to another fork in the trail and follow the sign for Queen's Garden. Is she trying to lose me? My head spins, and I fall against the base of a hoodoo. Three people are walking toward me on the trail, huge backpacks full of gear on their backs. One of them says, "You doing ok?"

"Yes, just stumbled over a loose rock. I'm fine, thanks," I tell him.

"Take it easy, man," he says, and they walk past me. "Maybe drink some water?"

I nod, but of course Jill has the water, not me.

I take a moment to breathe and notice the shadows are getting longer, and the light is softening, a welcome relief as long as I can find my way out of here before dusk. The trail is well marked, I'll be fine.

Jill knows I'm back here. She knows I've never been here before. She has the water and the trail knowledge. I can handle this. I have an attorney and a plan. And I have a few helpful recordings of my wife's confessions saved on my phone. We will not end things amicably, that much is clear. But hopefully, with the proof on my phone, we can agree to a standoff of sorts. The only thing left to do is finish the hike, head back to the lodge. Easy to find. Check on Erica. Eat dinner, alone would be just fine, hop in my car first thing in the morning and drive home, with or without Jill.

There will be no happy divorce. And she's smart enough to have only written down my sins in her notebook, not her own. But I have her own words of confession on my phone.

I wonder what she's told Dr. Kline about me. What did she tell her friend Michelle? It doesn't matter anymore, I suppose. Since I have a moment alone, I pull out my phone and Venmo my attorney Doug his huge retainer, paying from a credit card I opened a month ago. Thankfully, the transfer goes through. Jill doesn't know about the card, or my attorney. I don't want to know what she'd do to me if she found out about it.

Hands grab me from behind and shake me. "Boo!"

It's Jill. My phone drops from my hand onto the hoodoo's base and begins a quick and bumpy slide down the side of the cliff before it disappears from sight and slips into the abyss.

"Damn it!" I yell, my words echoing off the mostly face-less hoodoos.

"Oops, sorry," Jill says, both of us staring down into the deep canyon where my phone now lies. "Hikers will find it, I bet. They'll give it to a ranger, and they'll bring it to you. No worries!"

No worries. I'm so frustrated I could scream. "What is with you? You left me on the trail alone and then you circled back to scare me half to death, and made me drop my phone? What the hell, Jill?"

"You're so whiny, you know that. You remind me of your mom, not your dad," she says, hands on hips, feeling superior. "Here, drink some water. Calm down. It's just a phone."

I take the water bottle from her without a word and chug the rest of the contents. "I need to get out of here. Go report my phone has jumped over a cliff."

"If your mom hadn't been so whiny and nervous and jittery about your car hiding in their garage, about them possibly getting in trouble for being accessories to a crime, we all would have been fine," she says.

"I don't know why you're dissing my mom when you just caused my phone to take a dive from a cliff," I say. And then I realize she's trying to tell me something about my mom.

"I'm just saying, you have to agree with me, she made it all worse. And she almost cracked under pressure, remember?"

Why is she bringing all of this up? To torture me. To cause more nightmares, likely. "My mom was strong. Her only problem was that she had a conscience."

"I don't think that's what I'd call it. She was weak, you know it. That detective, he so much as told me one of the family members was getting close to giving up the car. And it was only year four."

I start walking on the trail. I don't care if she follows. I don't care about what she's trying to tell me, although I know I should. I don't care about anything but getting back to the lodge. I'll borrow a landline from Rhonda and call Erica. I'll file a missing phone report. Everything is fine.

I hear Jill's hiking boots close behind me, feel her breath on my neck. She's too close.

"Don't you want to know how I fixed everything?" She's using the singsong voice again.

"Leave me alone, *honey*," I say without turning around. I need my phone. I need to record Jill. Damnit. "Let's talk later, ok?"

"Nope! I'm going to tell you anyway! Right now!"

36
NOW

JILL

Jack keeps trying to get away from me, but I'm in shape, better shape than he is, and I keep up the pace. I'm right behind him, right where I want to be. I can't believe he's forcing me to tie us together even more tightly. He's giving me no other choice than to tell him more about everything I've done, we've done, to protect our marriage. But I'll take my time, of course.

"So, you were totally stressed out, weren't even excited that we had a baby," I say. "That wasn't ok. It made me feel totally alone."

In front of me, Jack puts his hands over his ears like a child. Really?

"Jack, stop that."

"I can't hear you and I'm not listening," Jack says. "We never talk and it's too late to start now. You know I loved Maggie from the minute she was born."

"Fine, I've got all night," I say, even if he's not listening. I take this time to look around. I did enjoy the trips here as a child, playing with my siblings, stargazing, roasting s'mores on the campfire. It was an innocent, idyllic childhood. Too bad I was neither.

I guess she just came this way, my mom often said. She tried to understand me, to help me, she really did.

But Jack's mom did not try to help us, not at all. She hated me, that much was clear. I remember the phone call. Maggie was three years old, chubby and cherubic, active and already a daddy's girl, likely for good reason. The phone rang, and I answered while Jack was busy bathing our daughter.

"I need to speak with Jack," Jack's mom demanded.

"Well, he's busy, but you may speak with me, Evie," I said.

"Please." She softened her tone and approach. But it wouldn't work. She'd already put herself on my bad list in my notebook, and it's very hard to move out of that column. Think of it like Santa's naughty and nice list, or if you will, a hit list of sorts. People I need to get even with, or something like that. Mostly harmless, you know.

"Look, whatever you have to say to Jack, you can say to me. I'm your daughter now," I said, wondering how she'd handle that one.

"The detective called. He was very threatening. Said he is working on a search warrant for our home. We can't have them search our property."

"No, that can't happen," I agreed. "What does Jackson suggest?"

"He's on his annual golfing trip with his best friends. I don't want to ruin that for him, not unless I have to. Please, have Jack call me when he finishes whatever he's doing. We need a plan."

"Sure. But remember, this is your fault," I said.

"What? Are you kidding? Watch your mouth, young lady. I've done nothing but help you, both of you, since you crawled into my son's life." I imagined her touching the pearls around her neck, taking a sip of her martini, up, dirty and with a twist.

"Crawled? Interesting choice of words, Mom."

"Clawed? Is that better. All I know is that since you appeared in Jack's life, his has been ruined. No job at the family firm, no more fun with his friends, no UCLA, no future really. Just you and a baby neither of you could afford without our help and some correspondence course law school. It's a tragedy. Call it what you want, but I know what you are, and I know what you've done."

The phone quivered in my hand as I shook with rage. How dare she? I saved Jack that night he killed Ted. I was the one who got him through college. Without me, he'd be nothing. Instead, he's a doting father, working at an ad agency and taking law school classes at night. And every morning, he wakes up to me, his loving wife.

"I'm the angel who saved your son," I said, controlling my tone as much as possible. "And you're the devil that is going to ruin it all. Keep your mouth shut. Stop taking the detective's calls."

"Don't you dare tell me what to do," Evie said, her voice quiet, threatening.

"You still think you're in charge, don't you? What an illusion. He's mine now, just like every son when they marry the wife of their dreams. You've been replaced. Have a nice evening, Evie."

I hung up. And that was the last time I ever spoke to her. Jack never did call her back, likely because when he asked who called, I told him it was a wrong number.

37
NOW

JACK

This trail seems to go on forever, much like the drive from Zion to Bryce. That's all because I'm stuck with Jill. I remind myself this is the end.

The sun is close to setting, and the shadows cast by the hoodoos are claustrophobic. I need to be out of this canyon and back on the ridge. And with one final switchback on the trail, I'm out. I've never been so happy to see other tourists, a paved path, and wide-open space.

I turn and look behind me, but Jill isn't there. After miles of her breathing down my neck, ever since my refusal to listen to anything she wants to tell me about fixing things, she must have backed off. That's great with me. I needed a break. I can only take so much of her and her threats, her lies. Her notebook readings. I'll pull myself together and get back in control in time for dinner. I will listen to whatever horrible story she wants to tell me then in the safety of the lodge.

Fortunately, I remember how to find my way back to the lodge. I walk along the edge of the canyon and try to appreciate the beauty. It is unlike anything I've ever seen before and I vow, someday, to bring Erica here and make happy memories. I spot the wooden sign pointing to the path through the woods leading to the lodge. It's almost dark now, stars dot the sky already and the moon is a sliver on the horizon. Chills zip down my spine as night falls. In the distance, the lights of the lodge beckon.

I emerge from the woods with relief and smile as I reach the hotel. I take the steps two at a time. Out of the corner of my eye, I see a candle flickering on the wooden table on the corner of the porch. I can make out the shape of a person sitting in a chair. Someone having an intimate dinner, perhaps.

I pull the door open to go inside, and Jill calls my name. I don't know where she is.

"Over here!" she calls. Jill is the person in the corner with a candle.

"I'm freezing. Going inside. See you later," I say.

"I'm having a vigil," she says. "For your parents."

If I wasn't already cold, my blood would have turned to ice. What is she doing now? "Why?"

"They died on this night, fifteen years ago." Her voice has that singsong quality like she's reading her notebook.

I walk to where she's seated. The candle is strong enough to illuminate the scene she wants me to see. A framed photo of my parents, on the last wedding anniversary before they died, has been placed on the table next to the candle. On the other side of the candle, the Story of Us notebook taunts me. I want to grab it and run, but I am distraught by the images of my parents, the reminder of their tragic deaths.

"You know I don't memorialize their death date, it's ghoulish," I say. A new chill rolls down my spine. That photo, that exact one, appears and disappears randomly in our house. Has Jill been prompting my nightmares, propelling them with props? I reach for the notebook, but she's faster, slipping it off the table and into her lap.

"Would you like me to read you another entry?" she asks.

"No, thanks, I'm going inside."

We lock eyes. A smart man would have been recording her readings all along during the trip, and I have been. But now, when I know she's going to make a confession, I don't have my phone because she shook it out of my hands.

"Sit now or you'll never know the truth about your parents," she says. "Now or never."

I take a deep breath, stare at the flickering light illuminating my parents' faces, and sit.

"Good boy." I watch as she opens the notebook. Instead of reading from the pages, she stares into my eyes. "I didn't really write this down, but here's what happened."

I drop my eyes to the photo of my parents as a violent shiver rolls down my spine.

"Someone had to do something before evil Evie ruined everything and sent you to prison," Jill says. "Evie's call that night made that clear."

"What call, Jill? What did my mom say to you?" My hands shake as I reach for the photo.

"It's not important. After you fell asleep that night, I snuck out of our apartment and took a drive. After purchasing a few things I needed at an out-of-town gas station, I arrived in Bel Air around three a.m. This time I knew better than to open the formal gates, as that had caused a ruckus when you and I drove the BMW in that night."

"Stop."

"Instead, I squeezed through a break in the hedge on foot, carrying my equipment, reaching the garage without setting off any trip lights. My adrenaline was pumping, that's for sure."

"Please," I say, finally looking up from the photo of my parents and meeting her cold blue eyes.

Jill says, "It was easy, really. My plan was simple. Eliminate the evidence. That the fire burned so hot, so fast wasn't my fault. Who knew your parents stored all that old wicker furniture and the lawn mowing equipment in the garage? That, plus your car, their cars, well, it was a tinderbox."

She isn't reading. She didn't write any of this in the notebook, of course she didn't.

"Your dad wasn't supposed to be home. He was on a golf trip, Evie told me that."

His friends told me he had worried about my mom, her state of mind, and returned home early from his favorite trip of the year.

She murdered my parents.

My heart pounds in my chest. I'm finding it hard to breathe. I reach for the photo, grab it, and hold it to my chest. Tears fill my eyes. I hear someone moan, realize it's me.

"You are a monster," I say.

"Takes one to know one, handsome."

"Why are you telling me this now? After all these years, why the truth now? Just to hurt me?"

"I wanted you to know you're not alone. We're both the same. You killed Ted, accidentally, and I killed your parents, accidentally." She shrugs. "Even. Tied together in crime."

"You just love hurting people," I say.

She smiles. "You always hurt the ones you love the most."

I stand, snuff the candle flame out with my fingers, and leave her alone in the dark, where she belongs.

38
NOW

JILL

Jack is so dramatic. Sobbing and moaning as if his parents just died. It's been fifteen years. Get a grip.

"I'm going to turn you in," he says, still clutching the photo of his parents like a shield.

"Good for you, and good luck with that. The fire was ruled accidental. There's a new home built on your parents' lot. Besides, a fire is only considered arson after all accidental causes have been ruled out. You'd have to prove I did it, but you can't. Besides, I was only destroying evidence to protect you, handsome. That it got out of control wasn't my fault. So, you're welcome."

I really do have to fix everything.

Jack stands, wipes his face on his sleeve, and walks away, heading inside the lodge. I grab my candle and backpack and follow him. It's time to change for dinner. And after, a little stargazing with the rangers. My parents let us stay up late here, just to see the stars.

When I enter the lobby, I spot Jack at the front desk, talking to Rhonda. Doesn't she ever go home?

"Hey, hope you guys can help with Jack's phone," I say, reaching the desk.

"We're in the process of reporting it missing. I'll notify the ranger staff. Do you have a computer with you? You can locate if for us," Rhonda says. "Or a watch that's paired?"

"No, unfortunately," Jack says with a heavy sigh.

"Well, it will likely turn up as most things that fall into the canyon do, one way or another," Rhonda says. "Besides, I'm sure you have it synced to the cloud."

"Oh, you know, you're right," Jack says. "That's so true. Ok, that's great. Thanks for reminding me."

Rhonda is so tech savvy, this one. Surprising. I smile at her, and she tilts her head.

"You look so familiar," she says.

"I have one of those faces. Strangers always come up to me thinking they know me, but they don't," I tell her.

Jack puts the photo of his parents on the counter, stands them up to face me. "Actually, Jill grew up in Salt Lake City. Last name Larkin. Do you know the Larkin family?" Jack says.

"My stars, do I! I'm a Larkin. I knew it. Oh, Jilly, you're the one they sent away," Rhonda says. "I'm glad to see you're doing well."

I try to smile at Rhonda, but I'm so furious with Jack I could kick him. I control the narrative here, not him. And when did Rhonda start working here anyway?

"So well. So happy and in love," I say. "Have you worked at the lodge long?"

"No, I started last week. Looking for something to do and I found it. And now, I've found you," she says.

This is so infuriating. I don't want my family to know anything about my life.

"Well, lucky us to stay here during your first week. Anyway, we need to go get ready for dinner," I say and wrap my arm around Jack's waist. He pulls away.

"Sure, Jilly. Have you called your mom? I know she'd love that," Rhonda says.

I answer with my best stare.

"Well, never mind me. Let me get this lost and found report filed. You two are having dinner with us tonight in the dining room. Reservations are in thirty minutes," Rhonda says.

Jack turns to me. "Why don't you go to the room, freshen up. I'll join you after we finish here."

I don't want to leave him alone with Rhonda, but I do need a hot shower. And I brought a special outfit for tonight's date. Jack seems to be back to normal, over the shock about the accidental murder. I mean, he should be. He thinks he accidentally killed his best friend. I accidentally killed his parents. We're even.

"Ok, handsome, I'll do that," I say and kiss him on the cheek. I grab the photo from the counter. "I'll take care of your parents, take them up to our room."

As I turn and walk away, I hear Rhonda tell Jack how sweet it is that he travels with a photo of his parents. I'm laughing as I walk down the hallway toward our room.

39
THEN

JACK

I don't remember much about the time when my parents died. I remember the funeral, double caskets, side by side, my beloved parents both gone. I remember Jill supporting me, literally, holding me up during the receiving line.

There were so many mourners. My parents were respected members of the community, pillars of society. But more. They loved me, stood by me despite my horrible accident and subsequent bad choices. In return, I jeopardized everything they owned, everything they'd built by hiding the evidence in their garage. I was the worst son.

"I should have turned myself in, all those years ago. It was an accident," I said.

"Stop, Jack, the past is the past," Jill said. She refused to discuss what happened that night, aside from telling me it was over, the past. That we had to move on. I guess I had, but at what cost? And now, my parents were dead.

"I should have taken Maggie over to visit them more," I'd said as we rode in the funeral procession following my parents' hearse.

"They could have reached out more too, Jack," Jill said, patting my hand. "This is not your fault. You had no idea they would die now, so young."

"I should have made more time for them. Should have played golf with my dad," I said. I knew he was disappointed in me for not getting into UCLA. And I knew my mom didn't like Jill, especially after everything that happened that night of the formal. My mom blamed her when I was the one at fault.

My parents loved me unconditionally, and I didn't make time for them once I married. That was the truth.

"They loved you so much, Jack. You'll always have those memories. And they knew you loved them too. Your speech was perfect at the funeral," Jill said.

"It would have been better if I'd said all those things to their faces, when they were alive," I moaned, losing my composure again.

"You're going to be ok, Jack. We'll get through this together."

"I don't know if I could without you." I meant it. My parents were my only other family. Now, it was just Jill and Maggie and me.

"You'll always have me by your side, Jack, always," Jill said as our car turned into the cemetery.

"Thank you for saving me," I said. And I believed it.

40
NOW

JACK

I wait until Jill disappears down the hallway. "Please, tell me everything you know about Jill Larkin," I say. I might sound desperate, or confused, and I know I look deranged, red-ringed eyes, hollow cheeks. I know, but I need someone on my side.

Rhonda takes a step back in alarm. I'm sure it's odd for her to have me, Jill's husband, begging for information about his own wife. "Well, I'm not sure what to tell you, son. She's your wife, right?"

"She is. But I don't know anything about her past. She would never tell me, like she was embarrassed by it or something. It would help us, strengthen our relationship, if I could understand what she's been through." I keep my voice calm. I'm just the loving husband. "It's ok, Rhonda. You can tell me."

"Well, you know, the family didn't discuss her much. She came from good, solid stock, leaders in the church, you know. Family of ten kids, she was just the black sheep, so to speak." She leans forward. "Between you and me, I heard the devil took her."

I involuntarily lean away. That would have been good to know two decades ago. "What does that mean?"

"Well, she just wasn't like the others. Did some bad things. Stealing, having relations with boys, even, some say, starting fires and killing rabbits and other critters. But that could all be made-up stories since she went away," Rhonda says. "I mean, who knows. She looks gorgeous, happy. She's married to a fine man. You have children?"

I nod. "Yes, one. A daughter. She's in college now."

"Wonderful. I'm going to call her mom Sheila and let her know the good news."

I nod and continue to agree with Rhonda's assessment of Jill, despite the fact the opposite is true. "You know, I'd love to get in touch with Sheila too. If you wouldn't mind sharing her number. I'll clear it with Jill, of course. Maybe we could have a reunion of sorts?"

"Don't see why not. Sheila and Curt are in the phone book," Rhonda says and writes a number down on a piece of paper, then slides it across the desk. "Let me go file that report."

"Rhonda, could I use that phone, please?" I point to the landline on her desk.

She shakes her head. "Can't let you use the lodge phone, it's policy. But here's my mobile. If you stand over there, under that black and white photo of the amphitheater, you'll have service, at least for a bit. You're going to call Sheila tonight?"

"Oh, no, need to check in with my daughter." I smile, grab her phone, and hurry to the corner as directed.

I punch in Erica's number, but it rolls to voicemail. "Erica, it's me. I'm using a borrowed phone because mine fell off a cliff. Listen, I love you, and I can't wait to be with you starting tomorrow night. And I have so much to tell you. I'll try you again, hoping you'll pick up this time."

I hang up and call her. Again, it rolls to voicemail. I'm running out of time. "Hey, it's me again. I want you to know, in case anything happens to me, that Jill killed my parents. The fire wasn't an accident, she started it."

Jill is walking down the hall toward me. She's wearing a long, shiny navy skirt and a navy sweater. The necklace sparkles. She looks as if she could be walking a runway, not dining at a lodge. I remember the phone in my hand, hang up, and slip it into my pocket.

I think about the fire at Erica's house yesterday. I tell myself to focus on Jill, to keep a neutral tone. I try for calm and friendly despite my dread.

"Wow, you look gorgeous," I say.

"Thank you. You need to go get ready. I have a very special dinner planned," she says. "I guess I'll go grab our table?"

"Yes, great idea. Order a drink and I'll be right there. Just waiting for Rhonda to file that report. She told me to look at all these amazing black and white photos while I waited."

"Very artsy of you, Jack."

"You know me." I notice she isn't carrying the backpack, but I'm sure she has the notebook with her.

"Well, I'll see you in the dining room. This will give me time to journal," she says and pulls it out of a purse I now spot, a purse the same navy blue as her outfit.

"Be sure to write about everything we've done today. It's been quite a day," I say. I start to walk to the front desk to return Rhonda's phone, but Jill grabs my arm.

"Nothing has changed, handsome. The past is the past. We are building a glorious future together. No matter what. And don't even think about digging up my past. Understood?"

"I won't," I say, but I haven't decided yet.

I have eight hours before I'm leaving this place, this mess of a road trip. I will need to learn everything I can about Jill, including her sordid past, to have enough leverage to keep her quiet. I'll reach out to her parents, find out the truth. To get free. If I'm unsuccessful, though, I will take my chances with the authorities. Surely, anyone who spoke to me and Jill would realize who is a danger to society, who is the one with so much to hide.

Jill's confidence is impressive, I'll give her that. But she's wrong about us.

And now that I know where she came from, who she really is, I hope she's given me a chance to find what I need to break her hold on me whether she realizes it or not. She never should have insisted we visit Utah. But she did. And now, I have the upper hand.

41

NOW

JILL

Rhonda exclaimed that I looked beautiful and would love to take a photo with me after dinner. I'm assuming that photo would then be texted to my mom.

"Sure, maybe," I said and continued walking.

Rhonda and her familiarity are annoying. I don't need family, not any more than I already have. I will not pose with Rhonda, nor will I allow any unauthorized photos. Likely it's too late though. Rhonda has our last name and home address from the hotel registration. We even had to tell her the make, model, and license plate number of Jack's car for parking. If my mom, or anyone else in my family wants to find me, it will be easy now.

But why would they? It was good riddance on both sides when I left. My final gift to them, no doubt, solidified that feeling.

A young man with a bad face of acne greets me. "Hello, Mrs. Tingley. We have a special table for two reserved for you."

"Thank you," I answer. How did he know my name? I follow the youngster to what does appear to be a great table in the corner of the room. Private and romantic. The dining room has been transformed from earlier, white tablecloths cover every table, replacing the red and white checkered ones from lunch, and crisp maroon linen napkins adorn each place setting. Still, something is off.

He pulls out my chair and I sit. "Say, how did you know who I was?"

"Oh, my grandma, Rhonda, she told me who you are. You're sort of a legend in the Larkin family, you know?"

I turn my attention to the menu. I'm feeling claustrophobic, and I will not have idle conversation about my legendary status with a pock-faced teen. Rhonda is on my last nerve.

"Well, thank you for the table," I say. I pull out my note-book and open it. He's still watching me. "What?"

"Oh, I'm your waiter, ma'am. Can I bring you something to drink while you wait?" he asks, eyes glistening.

"Oh, yes, you most certainly can. I'll have a vodka and soda, with lime."

He looks like he's about to burst he's so in awe that a Larkin would order such a drink. He's in the presence of a real-life sinner and he's loving it. "Ma'am, uh, we only have beer or wine, if you're looking for alcohol."

"Oh, I am. I'll have a glass of chardonnay. What's your name?"

"Curt." My father's name. Our family tends to reuse old names like we pass down clothes. "I'll be right back!"

Finally, I'm alone with my thoughts. I know Jack will pull on his big boy pants and come down to dinner. I know he's hungry, and besides, he must admit we're even now. Two accidents, and both long ago. Perhaps he'll want to know what else I've fixed for him along the way, or maybe he won't. Just to be sure he makes an appearance, I've taken the car keys. Also, he doesn't have a wallet as of now, or a phone. Limiting.

I turn to the first blank page in my notebook, startled that I have only a few more blank pages left. I'll need to purchase volume two soon. I write: *Aside from Jack's fragile mood, we had a marvelous day in Bryce Canyon!! Jack and I really had a chance to reconnect, hold hands, explore the hoodoos, and rekindle that love we had when we first met, before the responsibilities of life got in the way. Tonight, we'll share dinner in the historic lodge's dining room, drinking wine and sharing memories. He does still seem depressed—and he accidentally dropped his phone over the side of a cliff. I hope he wasn't considering a jump?—but aside from those things, I think this getaway has been good for him. I still worry and I'll keep watch over him.*

I sense Jack in the room and look up in time to see him storming to our table, hands clenched in fists. Somebody's upset that he's not going home tonight, it appears. I'm disappointed that is the choice he made, although I was one step ahead of him as usual.

"Don't you look handsome," I say.

He yanks the chair out across from me.

Curt the waiter appears with my glass of wine. "Sir, could I bring you a drink?"

"Sure, yes, what she's having," Jack says, not taking his eyes off me.

"Ok, well, you might consider ordering a bottle then because if you have more than a glass, well, it's a lot smarter to have a bottle." Curt is so clueless about the level of hostility at this table, it's almost endearing.

"Bring the bottle," Jack says.

"Please," I add.

"Yes, ma'am." Curt scurries away and we are alone.

"I want my keys, and my wallet. Now," Jack says. "You cannot hold me hostage here."

So dramatic, as usual. I close my notebook and tuck it away inside my purse. "Calm down. Heads are turning." Really the only person watching is Curt. "I'll give you everything after dinner. Eat with me. I read the chicken piccata is to die for."

Jack shakes his head. Curt brings the wine and makes a fuss over opening it. "Would you like a taste first, Mr. Tingley?"

Jack leans back in his chair. I smile.

"Sure, son, pour me a taste." He performs a dramatic wine tasting that would be better suited for Napa. Usually this is funny, tonight it's annoying. "Tastes great. The perfect complement to our breakup dinner."

"Excuse me, sir?" Curt asks.

My stomach flips. "Oh, my husband is joking. He always threatens to leave me when I order expensive wines, don't you, darling? Can you give us a moment, Curt?"

I don't know why Jack's so obstinate. We're on a reunion trip, and we've been having some fun. We even held hands. Was that all an act on Jack's part? It saddens me to realize it must have been. Right now, I need him to calm down. He's out of control and out of choices.

42
NOW

JACK

I'd ransacked the room when I got there, looking for anything I should have seen before and missed. Other little surprises Jill brought with us on the trip. More photos, perhaps? More threats hidden as mementos.

The only thing I could find was a framed photo of Maggie, the day she left for college. It sent chills down my spine. By bringing this photo here, on this trip, Jill was making a threat to hurt Maggie. Oh my god. I reminded myself Maggie is safe at school, far away from here, from this mess.

After a shower and change, I packed quickly. As I was about to walk out the door, I realized my wallet was missing from the side pocket of my luggage. My heart skipped a beat. I reached into the pocket of my overcoat hanging on a peg by the door. The car keys were gone too.

It could only be Jill. I kicked my luggage, stomped out of the room, and headed to the dining room. Along the way, I reminded myself to look calm and rational in front of Rhonda.

"Hey, Mr. Tingley," she said with a wave. "The rangers will be on the lookout for your phone! Remember, you have it backed up!"

"Yes, I do, of course. Thank you so much. I'm just so used to having the phone in my hand, you know," I said, rushing past her. "And I'm late for dinner I'm afraid."

For a moment, I'd considered asking Rhonda to put me in touch with Jill's parents. Tonight. But what good would it do to drag up minor childhood transgressions with people who have a strong faith, and conviction? Would they want to know what she has become now? Something, someone capable of far worse? Aside from upsetting them, Jill would be furious. I think I've sparked her rage enough as it is. And she, mine.

And now I sit, trying not to gulp wine, trying to figure out how the hell I get out of here.

Across from me, Jill is blabbing about the menu as if nothing is wrong.

"Why do you have a framed photo of Maggie here with us?" I ask. I'm leaning as far away from her as possible, while still appearing to be at the same table.

"Our daughter? I thought you'd enjoy having her along, I know how much you miss her." She smiles. "I'm just trying to think of everything I can to make you happy. I'm trying to fix things, don't you understand?"

"Stop trying to fix us. There is no us. Not anymore," I say, careful to keep my voice low.

"Don't be silly, handsome. I'm not trying to fix us. We're fine. It's you who needs help. Your chronic depression, inability to hold a job, your violent nightmares. You seem to be losing it a bit, to be honest. Remember how you were so dizzy yesterday? Maybe it's a brain tumor?"

"No. It's you."

"Ready to order?" The waiter appears out of nowhere again. He has the worst timing.

"Not quite," I say. "Give us a couple more minutes, please." The waiter nods and shuffles away.

"You really should just order the chicken piccata. It's the number one dish in the Yelp reviews," Jill says.

"Give me my keys. And my wallet. If you do, I'll stay for dinner."

"And if I don't?"

"I'll leave. Call an Uber. Call a friend. I have a lot of options." I'm not going to make a friend come get me, but I am considering an Uber. Bryce Canyon to Laguna Beach will be a hefty tab. And then I remember I don't have a phone either.

"You're bluffing. But it's cute. Tell you what, you stay, we have dinner, go to the ranger sky walk—it's amazing—go to sleep, and then drive home tomorrow. They can mail you your phone, or you can buy a new one at home."

My shoulders relax a bit despite my doubts. It sounds as if she's agreeing to drive home in the morning. That is the plan I have with Erica. I should not drive these roads at night, not this tired, not this worked up.

"Deal." I put my hand out. She hands me my wallet.

"Your keys aren't with me just now, but I'll give them to you on the sky walk. Promise."

I want to believe her, I really do. I don't want to involve Maggie or Erica, although I could ask one of them to call me a car service. I lock eyes with Jill. She smiles.

"We leave in the morning? Promise?"

"Yes, you get to go home in the morning, honey," she says. "Can we order? I'm starving."

"Sure," I answer. We're being agreeable. Things are going to work out just fine. I only need to make it through one more night.

43
NOW

JILL

It's nice to see Jack relax, enjoy his meal. Clearly, he thinks it's our last supper together, but he's wrong.

"How's your steak?" I ask. "My chicken piccata is unusually tasty."

"It's fine," Jack answers.

"Looks a bit more medium than medium rare, but nothing's perfect. Like us. We aren't perfect but we're great together, and we're a team."

He doesn't respond. Sits across from me like a pouting baby.

"From the looks of it, Maggie and her motley crew have vacated the house," I say.

"I cannot believe you have hidden cameras inside our home," Jack says. "Spying on your own daughter. Spying on me."

"She came home to spy on me, I bet she was trying to find my notebook. Admit it. You put her up to it, so don't act so innocent. You two always gang up on me. You're just mad I'm one step ahead of you, as usual."

"You scared the kids, turning on all the lights, the TV! Who does that? She's your daughter. Those are her friends."

"Watch your tone." I look around to make sure we aren't being overheard. "I just wanted them off the couch. You know my rule. No sleeping on the white couch. It's a simple rule to follow. And speaking of rules, you know you are not allowed to have a girlfriend when you are married."

"That's not the situation here."

"Right." He really thinks I don't know what's going on. What an idiot.

"Look, Jill, I'm not happy. You're not happy. I want a divorce."

My mind flashes to a photo of Erica McCann, ten years younger than me, athletic, a runner. I picture her and Jack together, in bed, and my rage simmers.

"No."

Curt appears and fills our wineglasses. "How's everything?"

"Couldn't be better," I say, but I'm glaring at Jack.

"Well then," Curt says and backs away. We could be a little off-putting at the moment.

"My attorney will be serving you with the papers on Monday," Jack says.

"No," I say again, a little louder. "We'll drive home tomorrow morning, make a session with Dr. Kline. We'll sort this all out."

"I'm not ever going to that house again. I can't believe you've been spying on us all these years," Jack says.

"You'll need your things, so you'll have to come home." Ha! Unless he wants everything tossed in a dumpster.

"Already cleared out what I want to keep," he says. "The rest—the house, the furniture, the memories—is all yours."

"How? When? I would have noticed, Jack." He's bluffing. He'll come home with me.

A park ranger steps into the dining room. "Pardon the interruption, but if you are joining the star walk tonight, we will begin in fifteen minutes. Thank you."

"I'm not doing that. You've gone too far. I'm going forward with the divorce, amicable or not. I think you'll decide we both benefit from a peaceful separation. But it's your call. I'm leaving either way. Please join them and leave me in peace." Jack waves his hand, and Curt hurries over. "We'll take the check please, and another bottle of this excellent wine to go."

"Yes, sir! The stars are great tonight," Curt says. "I'll be right back."

I don't care about the damn stars anymore. I want to know how he cleared out his things. They were all there when we drove off yesterday. And then I know. It was Maggie. That's the other reason she made the trip home. I need to review the camera video more closely. I've only been focused on listening and watching the first floor, protecting my couch.

I'm sure I'll see it on the bedroom camera. Maggie all over my room, her friends too, likely. Packing her father up, helping him start his new life without me.

And now, he's refusing to go on the night hike. Fine. I'll just make another plan.

44
NOW

JACK

I shouldn't have told her I got all my things out of the house. That was a big mistake. After all that's happened on this trip, that was too big of a move, too much of a reveal. I saw her face, the anger in her eyes. Now she knows I'm serious. And now I think she wants to kill me. Her plan was to do it on the star walk, I'm sure of it. Somewhere, sometime during the night hike to gaze at the stars, I was to meet a similar fate to my phone's.

"What a wonderful meal," I say to the waiter. He hands me the new bottle of wine and two glasses. I put one on the table. "Great service too."

"Thank you, sir." The waiter gives me a big grin. "Hope to see you back here again sometime. You too, cousin!"

The look Jill just gave the waiter, well, let's just say he was right to run away. He also should not join my wife on the star walk.

"Cousin?" I ask her. This is funny. "He's your cousin? The kid waiting on us. I love it. Why didn't you share that little piece of information with me?"

Jill pushes away from the table and stands. "He's not related to me. None of these people are."

"Rhonda seems to think differently. Why not embrace your roots? They might be a good support system, you know, after the divorce."

She doesn't respond. In the lobby, a group has gathered by the fireplace. A sign says Star Walk.

I keep walking, and so does Jill.

"Your group is meeting over there," I say.

Jill ignores me.

"Have a good evening!" Rhonda calls to us from the front desk.

I wave and Jill ignores her. This seems like a very long shift for Rhonda. But still, I hope she isn't off duty for a while. I'll circle back after the tour leaves and beg to use her phone again. I need to call Maggie and make sure she's back at school. And I need to make sure she knows her mom is a monster.

We're power walking down the hall to our room. I'm not going to let her lock me out, and likely, she has a similar idea. We reach the door at the same time. She inserts her key and opens the door. I push past her to be sure I get in.

"Geez, Jack, rude," she says. I watch as she takes her overcoat from the coat rack and pulls a white beanie on her head.

"I'm going on the star walk without you, I decided. I have the keys, so you can't leave me."

I can, and I will. "Enjoy. And be careful. I imagine it's quite dangerous near the rim in the dark," I say.

"Yes, it can be deadly if you make a wrong move. See you later."

I decide to wait a few minutes to make sure she is gone on the tour. I open the wine and pour a glass. I think about Erica and hope she's ok. I know she's dealing with a lot, and she has no way to get in touch with me now. Her ex-husband hasn't been an issue lately, I know, but now her home has been destroyed. And I worry about Maggie and the very real possibility her mother will try to hurt her someday.

I'll protect them both, but I need to get out of here first. Maybe I should call the police, confess to everything I've done and take my punishment. Sure, I could spend some time in prison due to my role in multiple property thefts. It could be worth it to break free. But what if Jill isn't punished? What if she gets away with everything? No, I need to stay out of prison in order to protect Maggie and Erica from Jill. I need to stay quiet until I have more evidence against my wife. But I'm leaving her, no matter what.

I decide to search the room for my car keys, even though I know Jill is too devious, too smart to leave them anywhere I can find them. After a fruitless search of the same drawers and dressers as before, I sit on the bed. Our ground-floor room has a small patio off the back. I open the door and step outside. The stars are, in fact, spectacular—brighter, more vibrant than I've ever seen.

I look out over the parking lot and spot my SUV where I left it. If I had my phone, I could use the remote entry feature, get in, turn it on, and leave without looking back. But I don't.

It's time to find Rhonda and a phone. Maybe my phone has been returned, although that prospect is remote. I saw how big of a drop it was to the canyon floor. A chill rolls down my spine.

I'm just glad I was smart enough to decline the tour tonight. I don't know how, or where, but I'm certain Jill intended for me to find my phone in person.

45
NOW

JILL

I watch Jack standing on the porch of our room, clueless as usual that I'm near and watching. I'm concealed, crouched behind bushes, so close I can hear him sigh. I'm so close, in fact, that I could reach out and touch him, if I wanted to. It's times like these when I wish I owned a gun. Just a small, feminine one. Discreet and dangerous, like me. But I don't. So for now, I'll just imagine what that would feel like.

I had planned two perfect endings to this little trip to Utah, depending on his loyalty to our marriage. In the first, we continued from Bryce Canyon, exploring Capitol Reef, Arches, the Grand Canyon. We made love, we drank wine, we talked and laughed and connected. In the second, his life ended when he accidentally fell from the rim at Bryce Canyon during our evening hike while stargazing.

I know now, for certain, Jack is leaving me for another woman. I know who that other woman is. I also know my daughter is helping him. He must be on to me because he won't go stargazing, even though he is staring at the sky this moment, albeit from the safety of our patio.

Well, Jack, this isn't how it ends, not the way you've planned it, that's for sure. You see, I'm in charge. And I like you alive, I do. You're my one true love. I'd do anything for you and I have decided to keep you. I used to think if I couldn't have you then nobody could. But I've changed my plans.

I smile as I look at my handsome husband, so close yet mentally so far away from me now. I'll change that, I will.

Right about now, though, if I said "boo," he'd likely have a heart attack. Poor Jack.

46
NOW

JACK

I reach the front desk, but the woman greeting me isn't Rhonda. It's a short, elderly woman with large, black-rimmed glasses.

"Can I help you?" she asks.

"Sure, yes, I'm staying here and I lost my phone on the trail this afternoon." I look over my shoulder to make sure Jill isn't around. "Could you check to see if it's been found?"

"Oh, did Rhonda file a report?" she asks. Her name badge says JUNE.

"She did, yes."

"Well, if that was just today, you won't know anything until tomorrow afternoon, at the earliest. That's when the rangers make a tally of all the lost and found and write up a report. Then they send it out to interested parties, like us at the lodge. Then, if we find there's a phone located, we call you," June says. "But you don't have a phone, so you should check back tomorrow afternoon."

The entire time she's talking, all I can think is I want to scream. I manage not to. "Thank you so much, June. I'm leaving early in the morning, so can I give you another number to call when you find my phone?"

"Sure." She slips me a piece of paper. I write my name, Erica's number, and a big THANK YOU FOR FINDING MY PHONE and hand it back to June. "Can I help with anything else?"

"Actually, yes, may I borrow a phone?" I ask. "It's sort of an emergency. I need to call my daughter, and well, my phone is gone."

"There's a pay phone by the gift shop, it may be working," June says.

"Don't suppose I could borrow your personal phone?"

"Don't have one. Don't want a brain tumor." June points to her temple. "Mr. Tingley, is it? Maybe borrow your wife's phone? She'll be back from the star hike in just about ten minutes."

"Yes, got it, thank you." Ten minutes. I check my watch. It's only nine thirty. I cannot spend the rest of the night in the same room with Jill. I can't. "You know what. We had a fight. I'm going to need another room. Do you have anything?"

"Let me check," June says, frowning. She busies herself at the computer, and I turn around to watch the door. Please hurry, June.

"Yes, we do, one room left. Should I charge the same card?"

"What a relief. Yes, that's fine."

"It's upstairs, and I'm afraid there's only a tiny window. It's more like an attic than anything," she says. "You'll find it up those stairs." She points across the lobby.

"It sounds lovely to me." I sign the printout in front of me and take the keys. "Thank you."

"Hope you get some rest and the two of you make up. Marriage is all about compromise, you know," June says.

Maybe a normal marriage is about compromise, I think. Not this one. This one has been filled with horrible secrets, debilitating nightmares, and lies. What would June think if I told her my wife killed my parents but I can't prove it? Is that something to compromise over? No, it's not.

I return to the original room, glad I packed earlier. I leave Jill a note: Departure time 6:15 a.m. Meet at the car. If you aren't on time, I will leave without you. ~ Jack

I am not sure yet how I'll leave without her since she has my keys, but I will figure it out. I grab my stuff and hurry out the door, certain at any moment I'm going to bump into Jill and an ugly scene will ensue. I check the hallway. It's clear. My new room is one of only five on the second floor of the lodge, but to get there, I must return to the lobby and cross it to reach the stairwell.

Besides June at the front desk and a couple sitting together in front of the fireplace, the lobby is empty. For once, I think, I may be one step ahead. I reach the room and slip the key in the slot, it clicks, and I push inside.

I close and lock the door, then slip the deadbolt and chain in place. And for the first time in hours, I take a deep breath. As I look around the room, I understand why it was the last one left. The room must sit at the top of the lodge, in the attic. A single twin bed and a tiny bedside table fit against one wall. A small shower and toilet are tucked into the other. Rustic, but all mine.

I sit on the bed and try to calm down. I'm anxious to get home, but as long as I know where Jill is, here with me, I know Erica and Maggie are safe. I need to call my attorney and get him working on the divorce documents. I'm glad I sent the retainer via Venmo before my phone was destroyed.

I stand up and begin pacing the tiny room, back and forth until I reach the spot where my forehead almost bangs into the ceiling. I think about my parents, about how they died. The investigators assured me it was painless, that they were overcome by smoke long before any flames reached their bedroom.

But still. How can they know for certain what they felt?

I wonder if I could call and leave an anonymous tip. Inform the police about what I know. Would there be any way for them to prove Jill's guilt? Can I testify against her once we're divorced, or are the spousal privilege protections still in place? Kicking myself again for not bringing my laptop, all I can do is pace and think.

I hear something outside my door. I stop walking and listen. Would June give Jill my new room number so we could reach a compromise? I don't think she would. I slowly walk to the door and put my ear against it.

I feel trapped, like any minute Jill will slip a key into the door and walk in. I think again of Erica, how I couldn't speak to her all day today. I hope I'm wrong about my fears that Jill could have something to do with the fire. I mean, it happened the morning we left for Utah. She was at the house when I returned home from breakfast with Erica.

I'm jumping to conclusions, giving Jill too much power in my imagination. She's not outside my door, of course not. There's a knock on the door and I jump.

"Yes?" I say through the door.

"Don, it's time to go," a woman says. "The whole gang is downstairs."

My shoulders sag in relief. I'm not Don, but I envy having a gang. "Sorry, this isn't Don's room."

"Oh, oops, so sorry. Have a good night," she says. I listen at the door until there is only silence.

No phone, no computer, no TV, and I didn't bring a book. I should try to go to sleep and hope the nightmares don't come. After I get ready for bed, I lie down on the bed and close my eyes. I remember the counting games my mom taught me when I was a boy, counting sheep at first and then, when I was older, counting puppies because I wanted a dog so badly.

Of course, my mom surprised me with a puppy for Christmas when I was eight years old. A memory pops into my mind of Buddy, my puppy, and my mom and dad and I sitting on the floor in the family room, the huge Christmas tree behind us, laughing and playing with the puppy. I hold that memory for as long as I can until flames and screams take it away.

I sit up in bed, heart pounding. I just need to make it through tonight. I'm fine. No one should be afraid of their spouse. But she has given me ample reasons. Everything will be fine as soon as I can get away from her tomorrow afternoon.

Maybe without Jill in my life, the nightmares will go away too? Maybe with the recordings on my phone, if my phone is ever found, and the threat of revealing who she really is, she'll let go of me. Erica and I will start fresh, and Maggie, well, I'll make sure she's protected at school. Somehow. Although I do realize, lying here in the dark, the only way to really feel safe from Jill is if she is put behind bars. But I don't believe that would ever happen. She's too good at what she does.

My only choice is to leave her and hope she'll accept a truce of sorts. I have to try, for Maggie and Erica, to get away safely.

47
NOW

JACK

I startle, open my eyes, and wonder where I am.

Bright light comes through the tiny window in my room. What time is it? I fell asleep without setting an alarm, without realizing my mistake, so consumed with worry. I look at the old-fashioned clock on the bedside table and have no idea if it's right. It says 10:30, but it can't be right. I hurry and get dressed, then grab my suitcase and rush downstairs.

Rhonda's at the front desk. "You must have slept well, Mr. Tingley!"

"What time is it?" I ask her.

"Why, it's 10:45."

My god. "Thanks, thanks for everything. I must go." I run out the front doors of the lodge and across the parking lot to my car. To where my car used to be.

It's gone.

I drop my suitcase on the ground and stomp my foot. That's when I see it. Tucked under a rock near where my front tire would have been. The envelope has my name written on it. It's Jill's handwriting, of course.

Dear Jack,

Thanks for nothing. I decided to skip the star hike and head home. I hope you had a nice last night of vacation. I'm sure you'll be able to catch a ride home from somebody. Nice Aunt Rhonda will help you, I'm sure. I think they may like you more than me. I know that's true because they know about me from all the family gossip, but they don't know you, how awful and mean you really are. They don't know you're a murderer. And to think, all this time, I worried about you and your depression, took care of you when all along you were planning to leave me. You even came on this vacation to try to trick me, make me think you still loved me. That's cruel, Jack. I won't forget what you've done to me, how you've hurt me. ~ Jill

Clearly, Jill is not happy.

I slide the note into the envelope, fold it, and stick it in my back pocket. I need to think. I need to get out of here. If Jill wrote this last night, she's already back home in Laguna Beach. What is she planning to do?

Oh my god. I need to warn Erica. I take a breath. Jill doesn't know where Erica is staying, so she's safe. Maggie is back at school, thank goodness, and she's living in a new campus apartment with the highest level of security. She and I put her mother on the restricted visitor form and spoke with the RA in charge of the building. This was about the same time I was questioning our marriage.

Maggie told me her worries, that I was trapped in a controlling marriage and one without love. My poor Maggie. I hated that she had to worry about her dad when that was my job, to worry about her. Her words hit my heart. It took me too long to take action. But now I am; I will. I hadn't even met Erica yet. Hadn't known I deserved real love. Truth be told, the ultimate catalyst has been finding Erica. Finding love. And now, I must believe Maggie and Erica are safe. That I will be able to keep them both safe.

I grab my suitcase and run back to the lodge. Rhonda is busy with a family: a mom, a dad and two small kids. I try to be patient, I do, but they are taking forever. I leave my suitcase and walk to the dining room searching for the waiter from last night.

"Curt!" I wave and cross the room. "Hey, I need your help."

"Mr. Tingley, sure, I'm just setting up for lunch, you hungry?"

I realize I am starving. "Yes, something to go, please, and I need a favor too." I lean close. "I need to borrow a car or get a ride to the closest airport."

"The Vegas airport is four and a half hours away, sir. When do you need to leave?"

"Now."

"Sir, I'd call the airport shuttle. There's likely room on the noon bus. Then you can fly on home."

"Can I borrow your phone? Mine is at the bottom of the canyon," I say.

Curt hands me his phone with the shuttle company loaded. After I make a booking, I call Southwest Airlines and buy a seat on the six o'clock flight. I'll be back in Laguna Beach by eight. I just need to make one more phone call.

"Do you mind if I call one more person?" I ask.

"Ok, sure, no problem, Mr. Tingley. I'll go get you a couple breakfast sandwiches to go."

"You're the best. A lifesaver, literally," I say.

I call Erica's number. It rolls to voicemail. I try a text: It's me. Jack. Please answer. I'll try again.

"Hello? Jack?" Erica says, finally answering my call. "What's happening? Are you ok?"

"Yes, I'm fine," I say.

"Are you on your way back? I got your messages. I've been so worried about you. And so scared. You'll stay with me at the hotel tonight, right?"

"Yes, can't wait to see you. I've gotten a bit of a late start, so I'll be there as soon as I can. Leaving now," I say. "I'm flying in from Vegas. I land at eight tonight."

"Ok, I can pick you up at the airport. I have so much to tell you."

"You too, honey. Look, whatever you do, if Jill contacts you or shows up at the hotel, stay away from her. She's unhinged and dangerous."

"You think she had something to do with the fire?" Erica asks. "Should I tell the investigators?"

"No, not yet. Let me get there first. I'm just not sure, and we don't want to poke the beast."

Curt reappears with a brown carryout bag.

"I have to go. I'll borrow phones along the way to keep you updated," I say.

"Be safe, Jack. I love you," Erica says.

"You too," I say and hand Curt his phone.

"This way to the shuttle, sir," Curt says. "I hope you have a safe trip. We'll mail your phone if we find it. And come back soon!"

"Absolutely," I tell him. Although I'm sure I'll never be back.

"Did Mrs. Tingley take your car?"

"She did."

"That's crazy. And left you here?"

"Yes, she did."

"Maybe you'd be better off without her. To tell you the truth, her family is relieved she's gone," Curt says.

"I guess I'm not surprised," I say. "Thanks for everything."

Curt leaves me sitting on a cold bench, waiting. Relief washes over me as, half an hour later, a green shuttle bus pulls into the parking lot. I'll be back to Laguna Beach in time to stop Jill from doing anything awful. I hope.

48
NOW

JILL

My eyes are blurry and red and my neck is tense, but as I pull into the driveway, I know it was worth it to be home early, alone, before Jack.

My home. No more sharing it, not anymore. I can do whatever I want now, here, and nobody can tell me no. I pull into the garage and push the button to close the door. I suppose I'll have to give Jack his car back at some point, but otherwise, the house and everything inside is mine. I try to feel excited for this fresh start, this reinvention that Jack is forcing on me. I mean, look at all the stuff I have all to myself now. I've always been a bigger fan of things than people. Except one.

Jack.

Who am I kidding? He is my sun and my moon—we are our own solar system. I'm not going to let him ruin us. Never.

I walk inside from the garage and instantly I'm sniffing, trying to smell signs of Maggie and her friends. Everything looks and smells in order, despite my daughter and the hippies descending on it. I walk into the family room and take a sniff. No smell of hippies here, thank goodness. No sage, no weed, no incense. I smell the white couch and check it closely for any signs of misuse. Everything's fine. Maggie is extremely lucky that is the case.

I'm already angry enough at her without adding any other reasons. I grab my suitcase and roll it to the bottom of the stairs. Jack was useful for carrying things. I'll do it myself. I pull my suitcase up one stair at a time and finally make it to the top. It is my own fault for going up a size when he had suggested carryon.

Once in our bedroom, I look around. It doesn't appear, at first glance, that Jack has moved out. His closet still has plenty of clothes, but when I walk into the bathroom and open his medicine cabinet, everything is gone. I rush to his bedside table and pull the drawer open.

Empty.

The next drawer.

Empty.

I scream and throw the drawer onto the ground.

That is the only reaction I'll allow.

I'm not worried, just a little surprised he pulled one over on me.

But I'll fix this. I always fix things.

PART TWO

TWO MONTHS LATER

BROKEN CROWN

49
NOW

JILL

I push through the door to the coffee shop and scan the crowd for Michelle. She's been my life support for the past two months, meeting me for coffee or coming over to the house to check in on me.

It's amazing to me that she is so true, so giving. I don't understand it; still, I appreciate it given my current situation. Things will change, but right now, the only one I have on my side is Michelle, though I am trying to meet new people.

I spot her in the corner, in a booth. As I walk through the tables to get to her, I notice a few people stare; four women at one table stop talking as I pass by.

I hate that I am once again a topic of conversation. The first time was when Jack ran for mayor and won. The next was when Jack lost. And now, it's because Jack left me. Why do his actions define me in these women's minds?

I can't take it anymore.

"Can I help you with something?" I stare at the ring-leader, the woman with the biggest wedding ring and the tightest workout clothes.

She blinks. "No, not unless you're bringing refills, Jill."

Her friends laugh, a nervous chuckle. It occurs to me they were all parents of children about Maggie's age. I should know their names, but I don't. And I don't care.

"Just wondering why you all stopped talking when you spotted me?" I ask. From the corner of my eye, I see Michelle frowning. Are my hands on my hips? I drop them to my side. "Am I the talk of the town?"

"Not really," Big Ring answers. "We feel bad for you, you know, about Jack leaving you. That's all."

I smile. "How sweet."

Another woman at the table says, "Men are so unreliable. And Jack, well, after that scandal while he was mayor, I knew he couldn't be trusted. Good riddance."

The one in a gray sweatshirt with a tall ponytail says, "I told Gary if he ever thinks of pulling something like Jack has with this new woman of his, well, I'd come after him."

I take a deep breath and remind myself these women are not my enemy. They aren't my friends either. They'll find someone else to gossip about soon enough.

"I'm keeping my friend waiting," I say, pointing to Michelle.

"Michelle's great," Big Ring says and waves to my friend. How does Michelle know her, and why?

I reach the booth, and Michelle greets me with a kiss on each cheek and a big hug. "You're even thinner than the last time we saw each other. Please tell me you'll eat."

"Well hello to you too," I say, slipping into the booth. Food these days is an afterthought, an annoyance. But she's right, I do need to keep my strength up.

"I'm just worried about you, that's all," she says. "And why were you chatting with Amy and her crew?"

"They're friends of yours?" I ask. My heart races with jealousy, despite my best efforts to stay calm. I like to imagine I am Michelle's only friend because she is mine. But I know that's not the case.

"We play tennis on Thursdays," she answers. "We're tennis friends. Remember, you used to play in the league too. So, really, how are you doing?" She waits a moment, and when I don't answer, she leans forward and whispers, "Brad ran into Jack at The Club."

"And what did Brad say about that?" I ask.

"Latte?" A waitress appears and plops the drink down in front of me. I stare at Michelle, waiting for her answer.

"He said Jack looked good, happy even. Not at all depressed, so that must be a weight off your shoulders. To not have to worry about him, I mean. You can move on with your life, and he'll move on too. You can both be happy."

Oh, Michelle. How sweet. "He has moved on *to* someone. A younger woman."

"Brad mentioned that, but it could be just a fling, rebound sort of thing." She tucks a strand of perfectly curled hair behind her ear. "But you don't want to get back together, do you? Brad said the divorce is almost finalized, per Jack."

I take a sip of my latte, which has too much almond milk, naturally. I lean forward and drop my voice. "The divorce isn't anywhere close to being final. Jack calls me almost every night, asking me to take him back."

"Oh, wow, ok, is that what you want?" Michelle's brown eyes blink with surprise, and new expectations.

"I have been through a lot with him, as you know. But in the end, we are meant to be together, don't you think? We make each other so happy."

Michelle tilts her head, brow furrowed. "I'm not so sure I agree. I mean, if he's happy now, and you're happy, well, maybe it's for the best that you two move on."

"You're saying that because Brad had one run-in with Jack? Jack could have been faking it, you know. He could have just acted happy, have you considered that? Because that's what he does. He's an actor, of sorts. He can put on a disguise of happiness. I mean, the whole time he was mayor, he seemed happy, but I told you how depressed he was."

"You told me that, yes. But that was after the scandal broke. Anyone would have been sad, especially since he's innocent."

"Yes, so innocent," I say. "Anyway, you'll see, soon enough he'll be moving back into our house, with me."

Michelle bites the side of her lip. She leans forward again. "Brad told me Jack has moved in with the woman. They're living together."

Somehow, I manage to keep my anger tamped down even as my stomach flips. I didn't know Jack was filling everyone in on his latest mistake.

"You know it won't last. It's a fling. A midlife crisis. He will be coming home," I say. Michelle doesn't look like she believes me. She should.

50
NOW

JACK

The short drive from our house to my new office takes me along a beautiful canyon road lined with a bike path, hiking trails, and the hint of the large Santa Barbara style mansions that echo the clubhouse design and dot the otherwise pristine landscape. We're only fifteen minutes inland from the coast, but it's a whole different, desert climate.

It's a wonderful new life. I tap the steering wheel of my new Audi e-tron, a nod to my concern about saving the planet and my confidence in my future, my earning abilities. I love my new job as general manager of The Club. I'm paid twice as much as when I was mayor and have one tenth of the constituents.

As Stanley said when I accepted the offer, "You're a natural. Keep the members happy and the staff in line and you'll be the club manager for as long as you'd like."

We were inside the formal conference room, tucked away near the grand entrance to the clubhouse. Just being there felt right. Everything about this step was right. I was finally moving forward, moving on.

"Thank you, sir. So much," I'd said, shaking his hand. He was the sharpest ninety-year-old I'd ever met.

"And Jack?" he'd said as I was about to leave. "I'm certain you're innocent in that money scandal when you were mayor."

"I am," I said, heart thumping. Not this again. "Thank you for giving me a chance, despite all the rumors."

"Some of the voting board members expressed their concern, on the record. They aren't as confident as I am," Stanley said.

"You don't have to worry. I promise. It wasn't me. I was framed." The argument didn't work during my reelection campaign, so I suppose it won't make a difference here either.

"They will be watching you, more closely than they should. That's all. Congratulations and welcome to the team," Stanley said.

I knew when I accepted the position that Stanley was taking a chance on me. I would prove to him I was the right choice.

My new phone rings. My old phone never was recovered from where it landed in the hoodoo world. The worst part is none of my data synced to the cloud, and I lost everything. I'm certain Jill somehow turned off the backup. I've had to start over with contacts, photos, everything. But with Maggie's help moving my things to my locker at The Club and Erica waiting for me at the airport, I had everything else I needed once I returned from that horrible trip.

"Hey, honey," Erica says. I picture her standing in our new kitchen, drenched in sunlight, smiling, happy.

"I just left. Do you miss me already?" I ask.

"I do, but I'm calling because I'm going to be a little late tonight. My new friend I met at pickleball wants to go to dinner, to get to know each other better. We're both new in town and you know I'm lonely for girlfriends. Are you ok with it?"

"Of course. I'll eat at The Club. Maybe ask a team member to join me. Bonding and all of that," I say. Since we moved in together, first in her hotel room and now in our new house in the canyon, we rarely miss a dinner together. It's probably healthy if we branch out, and I'm glad she's making friends.

"Thanks for being so understanding. Dean didn't let me do dinner out alone," Erica says. "I still can't believe he's been leaving me alone lately. It's so nice, not to be harassed."

"I know the feeling. We both had ridiculous marriages. But we're together now."

"And I'm starting to like this community." Her voice fills with sadness. "I'm committed to give it a go, for a little while, at least."

She misses living oceanside, while I quite enjoy the space away from Jill. But I'll live wherever Erica wants to live.

"We'll rebuild when we're allowed. You're fully insured," I say. "Don't be sad. We'll move back to the beach if you want to, just say the word."

"I love you," she says. "See you later tonight."

I pull into the formal drive of The Club, cruise around the circular entryway, and arrive at the spot reserved for the general manager. I feel like a little kid overly excited over the simple things like a reserved sign planted in the grass next to the newly installed electric vehicle charging station. I can't help it though. This is what joy feels like.

I hop out of my new car with a grin and click the charger into the port on the side of my car. I can't believe it's only been two months since I changed my life. I've never been this happy, ever. Of course, in the back of my mind, I'm worried about Jill. I'm worried because she's been so quiet. Why has she let me go? I wonder if she's simply biding her time, or the optimist in me thinks maybe, just maybe, she's found new happiness too. That's my biggest hope. With Maggie and me firmly and finally out of her orbit, she has room for new people, new friends, a new start.

I look up and say a little prayer to Mom and Dad. "Help me keep it this way."

51
NOW

JILL

My time with Michelle was not what I expected. She seems relieved Jack moved out of our home, has tried to move out of my life. She has it all wrong. I didn't share my plans, of course. I like keeping my thoughts to myself in those situations, and only promised we'd have coffee again soon.

I doubt that will happen, not for a while. She has disappointed me.

As I drive home, I think about Michelle's staunch defense of Jack. And she's correct.

Jack could never steal money from the city, from the taxpayers.

But I could and frame him for it, I decided.

Here's the thing. I hated Jack being mayor of Laguna Beach. The golden boy ready to save the day. He loved it, the way people would lean in and hang on every word he said. Only Jack could save the city from the big developers who want to ruin its charm, they thought. I personally think we need a little pizzazz, a little spiffing up, so bring on the developers. But I wasn't allowed to have a say. All I did was smile, try to pretend this was all a good idea, and clap when he finished speaking.

Jack was a crowd pleaser, that's for sure. Women loved him, crowded around him after speeches, like he was some sort of celebrity, which he's not. I didn't like sharing him this way. I didn't like all the new people who were coming into our orbit.

After he won, it was an avalanche of new people, new events, new responsibilities. New distractions. Less time with me, more time out and about. And more fights.

One night, after an especially long city council meeting his first year in office, Jack walked through the front door, tired, but whistling, wearing his favorite suit and a big smile. Dinner was cold, spoiling in the kitchen. He was happy, I was distraught.

"You could have called to tell me you'd be this late," I said as I stepped out from the shadows of our very dark living room.

He jumped, looked like he saw a ghost.

"Geez, Jill, you scared me," he said. "I hate it when you lurk around like that. Turn on some lights, why don't you?"

"Well, I hate it when you're late without calling. I imagine you dead on Coast Highway."

"Now why would I be dead on Coast Highway?" He shook his head and walked past me into the kitchen. "What's this?"

He pointed to what was roasted halibut with caper sauce and now looked like vomit.

"Your dinner. But it's ruined now. If you called, I would have put it in the fridge."

"You knew where I was." He sighed as he opened the refrigerator. "But ok, next time, I'll text or something. It was an intense meeting. I lost track of time."

I leaned forward closer to him, and barely caught it. The scent of her. The fact of her. I turned away and poured myself another glass of red wine.

He lost track of time because he was with someone else.

"How'd Maggie do on the English test?" he asked, still rummaging in the refrigerator. There isn't much in there. I like it minimalistic. Uncluttered. Besides, my family doesn't appreciate me enough to go grocery shopping.

I forgot to ask Maggie about the test, probably because Maggie and I don't talk. He knows that. "I have no idea," I said. "I haven't talked to her since last week."

"I'll call her in the morning," he said. He pulled out a carton of cottage cheese and a loaf of bread. "Mind if I have some?"

It was my cottage cheese, and I am not good at sharing. He knows that about me.

"Don't eat it all, ok?"

"I won't. There just aren't many options and it's too late to order delivery."

"And Jack, don't pull this stunt again, ok? Promise me."

He may have thought I meant not calling if he would be late, but that is not what I meant.

I was referring to her.

When he didn't stop, I decided to teach him a lesson.

I find shame to be the opposite of an aphrodisiac. I thought his spectacular mayoral downfall would be enough to end his dalliance. I was wrong.

52
NOW

JACK

I hear Erica walk through the door from the garage, and it's funny how excited I am. I'm like a kid again.

"Honey, I'm home!" she calls.

"Hey, welcome home." I meet her in the hallway and swoop her into my arms for a proper kiss. "How was dinner?"

"So great. You know, I haven't had a girlfriend to talk to in a really long time," Erica says as she slips off her camel coat. She's wearing a pink dress that fits her perfectly, sparkling diamond studs—from her ex, not me—and a big smile. "Dean kept me isolated. I let him."

"I'm glad you had fun. But I did miss you, not in the I-want-to-isolate-you way though." I want my future wife to have a happy life. One of balance and achievement, hers and mine.

"I know. You're the best," she says. We walk into the family room and sit beside each other on the couch.

It's so different. This. So different than anything Jill and I had together. To be fair, for years we had a tight bond, and common sadness, a child to raise, and exciting sex. But Jill and I were never like this. This is relaxing and warm. With Jill everything was edgy and exciting.

"Tell me about your new friend. Where is she from? What does she like to do besides pickleball?" I ask.

"Yes, her name is Joanie. We both signed up for pickleball lessons at the park in Laguna Beach. And now we're playing each other regularly. Both beginners, so that's why. We are terrible, but we have fun. She is from Texas, originally, but she doesn't have much of an accent, just a big laugh and smile. She's a redhead and so smart. I think she's lived in Orange County for two years or so. She's divorced, no kids. Doesn't know a lot of people, so we're a great match, off and on the court."

"Well, I can't wait to meet her," I say.

"That's a great idea. I told her I'd love to have her over for dinner this week, if that's ok with you?"

"Of course. I'd love to come watch you guys play too," I say. "After I get myself established at The Club. Leaving in the middle of the day to watch my hot girlfriend play pickleball likely would be frowned on."

"Yes, likely." She smiles.

"Would you like a nightcap?"

"Sure, and tell me about your day. Anything exciting happen at the world's most perfect club?"

Erica has taken to calling The Club "Club Perfect" because of the brilliantly green grass, expertly manicured, the hand-pruned flowers, the five-star cuisine. It is pretty perfect there. I make our drinks, a pair of cognacs, and walk back into the family room.

"I'm interviewing for a new director of food and beverage," I say, handing Erica her drink. "It's arguably the most important position after mine. A lot of interface with the members, daily and at special events. It's a big job."

"Any good candidates?" she asks.

"Actually, yes, I interviewed a woman today who has high expectation club service in LA. She could be the one. But I'll do at least five or six more interviews. Stanley and the board want me to be thorough. It's a test of sorts. Building their trust in me." I drop my gaze.

Erica reaches for my hand. "You didn't do anything wrong. You'll earn their trust in no time. Hey. I believe in you."

In my head, a little voice says this is too good to be true. I push it away and kiss my girlfriend.

53
NOW

———

JILL

I've been getting a lot more exercise lately, and I decide I should treat myself to lunch at The Club. Besides, I haven't seen Jack for more than two months, haven't seen him since I left him at the lodge in Bryce Canyon.

I'm looking forward to bumping into him.

I better hurry. I want to get there early enough that he'll have a chance to see me. I'd asked Michelle to join me, but she has those bratty twins, and they take up all of her daytime and most of her nights, it seems. It's fine. I am a strong woman. I can dine alone, and I'll pretend to be working on a story for the magazine on The Club. That way, they'll give me a great table by the window, in the grand dining room. I happen to know there's a big ladies golf tournament happening today, so there will be a lot happening. I'm lucky I made a reservation in advance.

I'm really very excited about it all. I hurry upstairs and change out of my workout clothes, then hop in the shower. While I'm standing under the water, I allow my mind to wander, to think about Jack and me.

I hated him as a politician. It wasn't good for our relationship. I wanted him to understand he was playing with fire.

I warned him too. He just didn't hear it. When he left the city-issued computer on his bedside table open, unlocked, and went downstairs to talk to Maggie when she called from boarding school, well, I had to do it. I was only going to look around. That's all.

Sure, I shared some files, sent a bunch of emails to Jack's email, printed them, then deleted the emails in the inbox and deleted file. But still, I wasn't certain I would do anything with them. I even wrote down some passwords, just in case. Electronic transfers were beyond my skill set—well, they *were*. And of course, I couldn't transfer city monies to me. That would be completely traceable.

So, let's just say I had to learn a lot before I could even act. I had been reading about those awful stories when a home buyer made electronic transfers for the down payment and swoosh, some nefarious creatures came in and stole the money. I learned how to become a nefarious online creature. Fascinating. And they still haven't found the $150,000 missing from the city's account. I mean, it's not a lot of money, just enough to make people talk, to make people doubt you as mayor.

I turn off the shower and watch the last of the water swirl down the drain. If Jack had ended it when I told him to, he would likely still be the mayor and the city would be $150,000 richer. But he didn't. He completely denied having an affair.

I knew better than to believe him, although he still thinks he fooled me.

What to wear? I'm thinking elegant, understated, chic. I'm thinking I need to go shopping, but for now, this will do. I pull a fall floral dress in muted browns and dusty pinks and slip it on. Paired with nude heels and an overpriced designer briefcase, I look the part of a high-end magazine writer. I remember to slip my laptop inside to look official.

After hair and makeup, the last touch is sliding on my wedding ring. I take a look at myself in the full-length mirror and decide this is as good as I'll get, and it's pretty darn good. I will drive Jack's car to The Club; he has a sticker and I don't. If I drove my car, I'd need to stop at the guard gate. Truth is, I just didn't use The Club much while we were together. But that is going to change starting today.

Dr. Kline tells me I need to get out of the house, socialize, go to lunch with friends. I guess this sort of counts?

The drive from my home in a gated community on the coast to Jack's new home in a gated community in the canyon is a mere fifteen minutes. But I'm not headed to Jack's house, of course. I'm going to The Club. Soon I'm pulling into the valet stand and handing over the keys to the black SUV.

"Welcome to The Club," the young man, says helping me out of the car.

"Thank you." I smile and nod. I see him looking at my legs. I like that.

"Here for lunch, ma'am?" he asks. "The front door is right behind me."

"Oh, I know. I'm one of the founding members."

"Well, I haven't seen you before, but welcome, Mrs.?"

"Larkin." He's getting too nosy, and I don't want him tipping Jack off that I'm here.

"Enjoy, Mrs. Larkin."

I walk slowly to the door, enjoying the attention. I loved it when Jack looked at me that way years ago. I've missed that type of look from men. I walk through the front door and into a formal hallway. The host stand is just in front of me, and beyond, through the windows, is the golf course, the pride and joy of The Club.

"Welcome. Do you have a reservation?" the host asks. She's familiar. I watch her take me in. "Mrs. Tingley?"

"Yes, hello, how are you?" I ask. Her name badge reads Jessica.

"Very good. Your ex-husband is such a joy to work for," she says.

"He's something else, isn't he? Would you let him know I'm here? No rush. Just have him come say hi when he's free. It's nice that we still have a good relationship, isn't it?"

"Of course. Is it a table for two, then? Let me take you to a special spot. Follow me." She leads me, as predicted, to the two-top at the window in the center of the formal dining room. Lovely.

"I hope you enjoy your lunch, Mrs. Tingley," she says and hands me a menu. "I'll tell him you're here. How wonderful to see you again."

Poor dear must not know Jack won't think it's wonderful, but that isn't my concern. I signal for the waiter and order an Aperol spritz. They're all the rage at The Club, I've noticed.

Once the waiter is on his merry way to the bar, I grab my briefcase and head to the ladies locker room to see if I can find anything interesting.

54
NOW

JACK

I'm in my office, reviewing another great résumé, when Jessica from the host stand at the restaurant knocks. I have an open-door policy and that means she walks in.

"Mr. Tingley. Mrs. Tingley is here. She's seated at table three in the dining room. She told me to tell you not to hurry, take your time," Jessica says.

If she noticed the color draining from my face, she doesn't say anything. "Oh, great, ok, thank you. I'm tied up now, but I'll try to stop by and see her. Otherwise, I'll talk to her later."

"Of course, sir, no problem," Jessica says and backs out.

Why is Jill here? The only possible reason is to try to ruin my life again. But she can't. She won't. I try to refocus on the résumé on my desk, but all I can think about is Jill. She is dangerous, unpredictable, and now she's at The Club. I stand

and start to pace my office, a space much different than the tiny hotel room at the lodge, but I have the same feeling in the pit of my stomach.

What if she's come here to make peace? I think about calling my attorney, asking his advice. I dial Doug's mobile and it rolls to voicemail. "Hey, it's Jack. Jill has shown up at The Club for lunch. Do you think I should go speak with her, or ignore the fact she's here? I could just be in meetings. Thanks for any advice."

I continue to pace, hoping my attorney calls back. After another ten minutes, I can't take it anymore. I straighten my tie, tell myself to get a grip, and head toward the dining room.

Jill sits with her back to me. She's wearing a beautiful, flowered dress—it must be new—her blonde hair shiny and curled, spilling down her back. If I didn't know her, I would think she was a gorgeous woman. But I do know. That's all a facade. My stomach clenches as I walk to her table and pull out the chair.

"May I?" I ask.

"Jack, how wonderful to see you. Yes, please, have a seat," she says. "You look good, handsome. This new job must suit you."

"It does. I'm really happy here," I say before I can stop myself. I know my happiness is not what she wants. "You look great too."

"Thank you. Dr. Kline tells me it's important to get back in circulation. Although I don't want to circulate. I want you to come home, where you belong."

She's drinking an Aperol spritz, and I stare at the orange drink like a beacon. "Look, Jill, this is my work. I can't have

you coming here, do you understand? The Club member-
ship is transferring to me. It's in the agreement. You have
the house, remember?"

"Oh, that silly agreement. We are so far apart. It will
take months before we agree to anything, and by then,
you'll likely be home," she says. "Can you join me for
lunch?"

I shake my head as a chill rolls down my spine. "No, I can't
join you for lunch."

"What a shame. How do you like it, living out here in the
canyon? From what I hear, your new home is quite grand.
Santa Barbara style with just the best kitchen ever."

"That is none of your business." How the hell would she
know about our kitchen, I wonder.

"You are always my business. But that's fine. I'm writing
a piece for the magazine about The Club and its new general
manager," she says. "Don't worry. I'll make you sound good,
despite your rather checkered past. I'm surprised they hired
you, I mean, a lot of people think you're a thief after what
happened when you were mayor." She's raising her voice.
She wants us to be overheard.

"Stop it, Jill," I say, forcing myself to remain calm, and
quiet. "I wonder if it was you? Was it? Did you frame me?"

"Little ol' me? Of course not, silly. I mean, do I look like
a hacker?"

I stare at her. No, in fact, she's a bad hacker it turns out. But
she started it. I just finished it my way. I never would have
taken that money if she hadn't left it in limbo in her efforts
to frame me, to humiliate me.

"I'll see you later." I stand and start to walk away.

"I'll need some quotes from you, for my story. You can try to explain it all away," she says. "We can do it now if you'd like. Jack?"

"Leave me alone," I say.

And this time when she calls my name, I keep walking.

55

NOW

JILL

My seafood Cobb salad is so good I don't want to finish it, so I'm eating slowly, picking at it, a bite of sliced egg here, a shrimp there, and enjoying the crisp sauvignon blanc my waiter says is the perfect complement. He's correct.

I'm also people watching. Some would say casing the joint. But that's not me, that's petty criminals. I'm just taking it all in, all the people, all the good fortune amassed here.

"Can I bring you anything else, Mrs. Tingley? My shift is about up," my waiter says. I check the time. Oh my, it's almost two o'clock. I've had a very long lunch.

"Just the check, please. Oh, and a copy of The Club's newsletter if there's one handy?"

"Absolutely," he says.

I turn my attention back to the outside patio, where gaggles of women golfers are gathering after finishing their rounds. They all seem so happy, sunburned in some cases, and carefree. I suppose they are. They are the lucky ones. Members of this exclusive club, pampered and privileged. I imagine they eat lunch here where I'm sitting at least once or twice a week. Their maids and nannies take care of most everything else, while they play, and eat out, and shop. That was supposed to be my life, but his parents, well, they disappointed to say the least.

"Here's the newsletter, Mrs. Tingley. It's been a pleasure serving you today."

I give him my brightest smile and wish I'd asked his name. "Thank you."

The newsletter reveals a treasure trove of opportunity for me just this week alone. In addition to today's Ladies Member-Guest Tournament, there is the Annual Fashion Show and Luncheon tomorrow, and it's only $350 per person. Just charge it to your member number. How exciting. I haven't been to a fashion show in ages—well, ever. I keep reading the newsletter and bingo: Saturday night, it's dinner and dancing to all my favorite 1980s tunes. Well, that might be awkward without a group, but we'll see. If I need extra time here, I'll do it.

I sign the lunch bill by adding my member number and a generous tip. Jack will be pleased I'm treating his employees so well with his money. Ha.

On my way out I stop by the hostess stand, and Jessica is still here. "Hi, would you be able to sign me up for a couple events?"

"Of course, Mrs. Tingley," she says. And just like that, I'll be at the fashion show tomorrow and the dance party Saturday night. "We'll see you tomorrow!"

I am beginning to love it here at The Club. As I step outside, the helpful valet already has my car—well, Jack's car—pulled around and waiting for me.

"Here you are, Mrs. Larkin," he says. I'm so happy there is a strict no tipping policy out here because I don't have a penny to my name at the moment, although I will be changing that. I think of the extra weight in my briefcase and smile.

"What great service, just exceptional," I say. "I'll be back tomorrow."

"Wonderful. See you then," he says and closes my door.

I think he might be flirting, but that's just fine with me. Harmless but ego boosting until Jack finds his way home.

I think about Jack as I drive home in his car, with a quick detour. The gates of the clubhouse are the same gates for the residential streets surrounding it. Once you're in, you're in. And I am, so I may as well have a look around.

The winding road takes me up above The Club and reveals massive homes set on huge lots. I know most of these homes have their own pools, pool houses, sprawling yards, and outdoor kitchens. And as I drive slowly past Erica's home—the property is in her name because a woman can never be certain about her new man, and I admire that sentiment—I see a European-influenced sprawling estate.

According to the listing details I read, you enter through a fireplace-warmed gated courtyard. Oh, there it is. I pull over on the curb and pull up the listing on my phone. *Timeless, authentic details in a garden setting. The resplendent interiors span 5,000 square feet of elegant living. An abundance of French doors beckon guests to explore the grounds including a pool, a spa, and an outdoor kitchen with two sinks! Back inside a wine cellar, formal dining room, and chef's kitchen with butler's pantries are sure to encourage ambitious culinary endeavors and intimate gatherings. Enjoy an inspired lifestyle experienced by a fortunate few.*

So grand. Jack better be honing his culinary endeavors is all I have to say, although his girlfriend seems to love cooking, so maybe this is perfect for her. I watch as a white Mercedes SUV turns out of the winding driveway.

I pull away before the driver can see me.

Oh my. It's almost 4:00 p.m. Where has the day gone? I'm meeting a friend at five o'clock for cocktails and a beach walk.

I drive too fast along the winding canyon roads and make it back to my home in record time. I run upstairs, change into beach attire—sweatpants, matching sweatshirt, flip-flops— and scrub off most of my makeup. I do my hair. At the last minute, I remember to take off my jewelry. I rush downstairs and out the door, this time driving my car.

56
NOW

JACK

Ever since Jill appeared at The Club yesterday, I've been on edge. I know that's what she wants me to feel. The whole time we were married, she never came here unless I suggested it. This was my place for golf, for fun, always. And then, out of the blue, she drops by for lunch. And from what I heard from her waiter, Pete, she stayed until almost two in the afternoon.

She's up to something. My attorney tells me there is nothing I can do legally to stop her from coming here. She is a member until our divorce is final, and it's not. I am allowed to send her a bill for her expenses and hope she pays it.

I laughed at that suggestion, along with the size of the tip she added to her lunch bill when she knows it's a no tipping club. She doubled the cost of lunch and added that for the tip. Pete, being a nice kid, told me he deleted the tip but wanted me to know how nice Mrs. Tingley was to him.

There's a knock on my door. "Come in."

Stanley, the board president, makes his way inside my office with the help of his cane. I hope I can get around that well when I'm pushing ninety years old. "Hello, Jack."

"Stanley, sir, please have a seat." I usher him to the comfortable club chair in the corner of my office. "What a nice surprise!"

"I'm just here checking in on you. Have you found our food and beverage director yet?" he asks. "As you know, Brian's last day is Sunday. I'd hate to imagine the chaos that will ensue if we don't have someone hired."

I grab the résumé of the candidate I've been interviewing and present it to Stanley. "This is the person we should hire. She's seasoned, has glowing recommendations from her previous employer. She's ready to start tomorrow." I'm so proud of myself for finding Sandra. We've hit it off, both on the phone and during our in-person interview. She's Zoomed with five of the board members, as have the other two candidates.

"The board seems to be leaning toward the man, the one from Seattle," Stanley says. "They like Sandra, but they're worried about her time commitment, she has young children."

"That's sexist and discriminatory. We are better than that at The Club, aren't we?"

Stanley sighs. "Yes, we are better than that now. Please extend the offer to your candidate. Thank you, son."

Relief washes over me, and something else. Confidence. Stanley respects my choice, trusts me. As he leaves my office, my assistant appears in the doorway.

"Jack, one of the guests at the fashion show this afternoon wants to see you. She's distraught, and well, here she is," my assistant shrugs as a tearful woman pushes past Stanley to barge into my office.

"I hear you are the manager?" she asks, pointing a long, red fingernail toward my chest. Her eyes are flashing fire.

"I am. Can you please have a seat? What can I help you with?" I say, gesturing toward the chair across from my desk.

"I don't want a seat! I want to know how I was robbed during a fashion show at your club?" She holds out a large designer purse and opens it. "All of my things are gone. My travel jewelry—I just flew in from Rome last night—my wallet with thousands of dollars of cash, my makeup bag. Everything!"

"There must be some mistake. Where was your handbag?" I ask.

"On the floor, under my seat. My friend brought me as her guest. We watched the show and ate lunch, and just now, when I stood to leave, my bag was empty. Do you understand?"

Behind angry woman number one, just outside my office door, is angry woman number two.

"I've been robbed!" she yells.

I turn to my desk and reach for the phone, dialing the police, my newfound confidence draining from me as quickly as it had appeared.

"We will get to the bottom of this," Stanley says to the angry women.

"What kind of club is this?" the woman in my office asks.

"An exceptional one, madam," Stanley says. "Nothing like this has ever happened before."

And then Stanley looks at me with what can only be called disappointment. And I know, no matter what happened today, I will end up being blamed.

57
NOW

JILL

I had to leave the fashion show early today because I have dinner plans tonight. When Dr. Kline said to get out and about, he had no idea how busy I could become. What a week!

I'm home now, getting ready for what can only be described as a very special evening. I'm tasked with bringing the salad, and that's easy because my two hydroponic towers are bursting with greens and edible flowers, including the bright orange and yellow marigolds. They're almost too pretty to pick. Almost.

I rummage around in my kitchen—not equipped with two butler's pantries; a kitchen that does not inspire grand culinary feats—and pull out my favorite salad bowl. It's wooden, seasoned with use. From the cupboard, I pull out my seeds and nuts that add a little extra something to the dish. And then I go outside to clip the greens.

I have a flashback to the last meal I served Jack here at the house, the night before we drove to Utah. It was a test run of my salad, an experiment of sorts as I added new ingredients. But he refused to eat the salad, his first little act of defiance, a foreshadowing of the trip. That was fine. I ate his and mine, and it tasted great. This time I'm going to double the seeds. It will be perfect.

Once the salad is prepared, I make the dressing—olive oil, fresh squeezed lemon juice, honey, salt and pepper—and pour it in a mason jar. The salad is ready to go, and so am I. I've again scrubbed off most of my makeup I wore to the fashion show at The Club and gather my hair into a high ponytail. I leave all my jewelry at home, upstairs in the bedroom.

I leave the other things in the trunk of Jack's car.

I carry the salad and fixings to my car, and as I drive, I'm humming. The song is the one that was playing at The Ivy the night we were engaged, but I don't remember the words. I just remember how happy I was that my dreams were all coming true.

I read in a self-help book that it's up to you to make your dreams come true. And I did, with Jack. He is the only person I've ever wanted, the only one I need. He feels the same, he's just gotten a little confused. I park my car in the community adjacent to Erica's, and walk the trail connecting the two. I stand in the front yard of the home I told Erica I live in. I don't, but no need for her to know that, right?

Soon enough, she pulls up in her shiny new Range Rover and I climb in. Kisses kisses all around, awkward with the

Hollywood-white, snap-on veneers I wear as part of my disguise for her. It makes me slur in all the right ways. In addition to my red hair, I pencil on a mole just above my lip. And pop in contacts that make my blue eyes turn brown. My transformation is complete, and if I might say, brilliant.

I smile a big, toothy, too-white grin. "Thank you so much for picking me up. I'm not sure what happened with my old Mercedes. But anyway, thank you," I say.

"Of course. No problem. You live so close. We should be walking every morning, and then playing pickleball."

"Oh, yes, that would be fabulous," I say as we pull into her driveway.

"I'm going to have you come in the front door, like a proper guest," Erica says.

"Oh, how fun," I exclaim. Things in the canyon are a little more eerie at night. There are shadows, and pockets of complete darkness, unlike where I live near the beach. There is no space at the ocean, only house after house after house. Here, the lots bump into darkness, privacy and peace, theoretically.

"There's been a little something happening at the clubhouse tonight. Police are everywhere. Did you hear anything about it?" Erica asks as we walk toward her front door. Their front door. You can't help but admire the beauty of the home at night. Perfect landscape lighting, a gurgling fountain, and plenty of room to park. I can't wait to walk through the fireplace-warmed gated courtyard to enjoy the double-high rotunda crowned by rich wood millwork.

And I do. It's much better than the photos, even.

"You know, I thought I noticed the lights of police cars in the canyon, but I was so excited to be coming over, I didn't give it much thought," I say, realizing she thinks I live in this community where she picked me up. Ha.

Erica glows as she opens the front door. "Joanie, I'm so glad you could come to dinner! Welcome to my home."

"The pleasure is all mine," I say with a slight Southern accent. I'm impressed with my peekaboo hair. I learned how to do it on a popular YouTube channel. I dyed the underlayer of my hair red so when I pull it up into a high ponytail I look like a redhead. When my hair is down, I am a blonde. Fun! "Your place is gorgeous!"

"Well, come on in. I can't wait to show you around. And the salad looks great," she says, taking it from my gloved hands.

58
NOW

——

JACK

I've been told to remain in my office, and that is what I will do. Erica was understanding and said not to worry about hurrying home. Her friend is coming over for dinner, and they are more than happy to have a girls' night.

Jessica dropped off a club sandwich a few minutes ago and I take a bite, despite the fact my hunger is gone.

My phone rings.

"Mr. Tingley, this is Detective Donnelly. Could you join us, please, in The Club's ladies locker room?"

Do I have a choice? "Of course, be right there."

Fortunately, Stanley has gone home for the evening. I am instructed to call him with any developments. In his place, I'm stuck with the vice chair of the board, a grumpy man named Sid who never liked me, never trusted me. He voted against my becoming general manager, and he's here to oversee my downfall.

I encounter him outside my office, sitting in a club chair, drinking a scotch on the rocks.

"Where do you think you're going, Jack?" Sid asks. "You must stay at The Club until this is resolved."

A golden prison.

"Thanks for the reminder, Sid. The police asked me to join them, so that's where I'm going." I walk past him without another word.

I feel him following behind me like my prison guard. Fine. I have nothing to hide.

I reach the ladies locker room and knock on the door. Detective Donnelly opens it.

"Come in, Mr. Tingley. Who's that behind you?" the detective asks.

"Sid, he's on the board."

"Well, let's leave him out of this for the moment," he says and closes the door behind me. Too bad, Sid.

"What's going on? No one has told me anything," I say.

"Well, it appears there have been a series of thefts here at The Club in the past two days," Donnelly says. "It also seems to be an inside job."

"What? That's impossible. It doesn't make sense. We have the best club staff in the country."

"We're going to need to talk to every staff member who had access to this locker room, and to the fashion show event."

"Why the locker room?"

"It has come to our attention that several members and guests of the Ladies Golf Invitational had items stolen from their lockers," Donnelly says. "Some of them didn't realize it until the fashion show fiasco today. Two of your members lost significant pieces of jewelry."

My heart beats wildly in my chest, but I try to find any reason, anything that might explain what is happening. Anything that doesn't point to the one person I know who could do such a thing. I can't turn Jill in. She'd come after me, and likely frame me for all of this. I need to protect Erica. And Maggie. And my job. I can't let her ruin my new life. I need to handle her privately. I need to beg her to stop while her sights are just on me. I just want peace. Jill and I will reach an agreement. Nobody else can be hurt. My heart thumps in my chest.

I realize the detective is staring at me.

"Are you certain this isn't just a group panic? Women who have misplaced things and now are deciding they've been stolen?" I ask. "I mean, I know the two women at the show were victimized, I spoke with them. But the locker room?"

"We are certain there have been multiple robberies that have taken place in the past few days," he says. "Mr. Tingley, if you have any information about what is going on here, now is the time to tell us. It will be easier for you that way."

This can't be happening, my brain says. But I look into the detective's face, and I realize it is.

I tell myself Jill can't be behind this. I know she must be.

"I don't know anything, nothing at all. But I'll do anything you ask to find the perpetrator and bring them to justice."

The detective makes a small snort and says, "That will be all for now, Mr. Tingley. Please do stay in your office until we tell you it's alright to leave."

I turn and walk away without speaking. They think it's me. I think it's Jill. I hope to God they find out it's someone else.

59
NOW

JILL

I really cannot get over how beautiful this house is. I am even beginning to see the charm of living in the canyon instead of near the ocean. The sky is sparkling with stars, much brighter than what we see at the coast because of all the light pollution. I mean, it's no Bryce Canyon sky, but it's nice.

"And that's the end of the grand tour," Erica says.

"It's gorgeous. Everything y'all have done," I say.

"Well, it came this way. I bought it furnished and all, because you know, the fire." Erica sighs, and her eyes fill with tears.

"I'm so sorry." I wrap my arm around her. I hate that we are standing in the master bedroom. I hate that Jack makes love to her in here, on that bed. "Let's eat. I'm starving. How about you?" I need to move her along.

"Yes, of course, let's," she says, wiping under her eyes and leading me back down the hall, down the grand stairs, through the overdone entryway and back to the kitchen. It's a hike just to get around in here. Good step counts every day, I suppose.

"I hope you like salmon," Erica says, pulling a perfectly cooked dish out of the oven. My stomach growls. I wasn't lying about that.

"I do. It will go so well with the special salad I brought." I pull my salad bowl out of the butler's pantry refrigerator—it was the only item in there, I note.

I return to the kitchen island and watch as Erica serves up two plates. "Sorry but it looks like my boyfriend has to work late tonight," she says. "He really apologizes for missing dinner with you. He'll try to be here before you leave."

"Oh, please don't give it a second thought. We'll meet someday soon, I'm sure of it," I say, tossing the salad. As I work with the different Ziploc bags of ingredients I've brought, I am careful to sort and select what I'll add to her plate and what part of the salad goes on mine. I dish her salad first, placing a special white flower on top.

"Here you go," I say.

"That's just lovely. I want to take a photo," she says. "Post it on Instagram!"

She knows I hate social media. I've made that quite clear even as I've enjoyed her daily stream of oversharing.

"No. Remember our rules?" I say it with a smile. "I don't want any part of it, not even my salad to make an appearance."

"Ok, fine, but I'm going to change your mind eventually," she says. I follow her to the large round table. The view is of the swimming pool.

"You won't." I sit across from her. When she looks confused, I add, "You won't change my mind about social media. Why would I share my personal life with strangers? I don't like anyone knowing what I'm up to."

"Not even a friendly game of pickleball, with just little old me?"

We do have fun playing. After meeting at the one pickleball lesson we both took through the city a few weeks ago, I convinced her we'd have more fun playing just the two of us. I knew she was getting into pickleball because she posted on social media about signing up for the city's beginner lessons. Not smart, Erica, telling strangers what you're up to. I made sure to become her buddy that first lesson, and from then on, we just played together on our own. So much more fun, I told her. She bought it, as they say, hook, line, and sinker.

I smile. "Nope, not even then." I look across the table at my hostess. She is so innocent, and warm. It's a shame really that she got involved with Jack. Otherwise, she's a very nice person.

"Oh, I almost forgot the wine," she says. "Be right back."

If I didn't know better, I'd think she was trying to stall.

But I do know better.

Erica thinks we're friends. Pickleball playing, beach walking, dinner sharing friends. She is, of course, very wrong.

60
NOW

JACK

Sid walks through my office door with a bit of a tilt. I have no idea how many scotches he's enjoyed while I was being cross-examined by Detective Donnelly. I straighten my back and get ready for his attack.

"What did the cops want?" he asks, slurring.

"Nothing, just a tour of the locker room."

"Nah, that's not true, they wanted to question you." He drops into the chair across the desk from me.

"You know, Sid, there's no reason for you to be here. I have this entire situation under control." We both know I'm lying, but why is he here?

"Someone needs to represent the board. Besides, my wife is in Maui, and I live just up the street. I don't have anything better to do than watch you squirm." He smiles, chuckles, pleased with himself and his perceived power over me.

"I'm not squirming." But I do decide my tie is choking me. I yank it off and drop into my desk chair.

"You know I voted against you, don't you?" he asks.

I don't answer him.

"Blackballed you, or tried. Stanley said you were a good man, a good mayor, and that you weren't responsible for the theft of city money. But the money hasn't been found, has it?"

"I don't know. I'm no longer mayor. But I do know I didn't steal money from the city." I lean forward and place my elbows on my desk. I look down at my sandwich and push it away.

"We've never had anything like this happen in the entire history of The Club."

"I know that," I say.

"You're hired, and you've been here like two months, and this happens."

I shake my head. Nothing I can say will change his mind. Not until the true culprit is caught—if they are. Like the city money situation, the absence of a conviction leaves a cloud of suspicion over my head. A cloud I can't shake.

"If you'll excuse me, I'd like to make a phone call," I say, standing up and pointing to the door.

"To your lawyer?" Sid asks. He stands up. "That's probably a good idea."

"Fuck you, Sid." I can't control it anymore.

"What did you just say to the board vice chairman?"

"I said have another scotch, sir."

"That's better. I think I will do just that." Sid slams my door closed behind him.

I pick up the phone to call Erica, but I don't want to upset her with all of this. I'll let her enjoy dinner with her friend. She'll hear all about this soon.

I write her a text: I love you. Hope you're having fun. See you soon. xo

I wait for her response, usually quick, usually an emoji.

Sure enough, Erica responds: Love you too. Having the best time. Don't rush. Xo

Well, at least someone's having fun tonight. For a moment, I think about calling Jill. Maybe we can work something out. Maybe she could give me all of the stuff she stole from The Club and I could *find* it. I could be a hero. Maybe I could pretend I wanted to get back together? All she wants is for me to come back home. This isn't the way to get me back.

I try to eat a bite, but my stomach turns. This must be an inside job, I think. But it's not as if one of The Club's employees is a thief, and unfortunately for me, he or she waited until I was hired to begin their robbery spree. No, that's just not likely.

Detective Donnelly will find a suspect. Sure, he suspects me now, but not for long. I have witnesses, a packed calendar of interviews, and other matters during the time of the robberies. I didn't attend the fashion show, didn't even peek in to see how it was going.

I open my computer and type in my member number and pull up my account. In addition to Jill's lunch yesterday, she purchased a ticket to the fashion show. My pulse quickens and sweat rolls down the back of my neck. Jill went to the fashion show, or at least bought a ticket for it. I didn't see her at The Club today, but that doesn't mean she wasn't here.

Oh, Jill. You really are incredible. And incredibly dangerous. I will not be the one who turns you in, as you know. My only option with my soon-to-be ex-wife is to keep her close, exactly where she wants to be.

At this moment, I'm beginning to think I'll never break free.

61
NOW

JILL

"Oh, Joanie, that's hilarious," Erica squeals. She's finished her salad, most of her salmon, three glasses of wine (I'm taking tiny sips of mine), and now whatever I say is the funniest thing she's ever heard.

It's nice to have such an appreciative audience.

"Well, the fish was phenomenal," I tell her. I stand to begin clearing the plates.

Erica tries to stand too but falls back into her seat. "Whoops."

"You sit. I'll clear."

"Boy, I feel really drunk, like really, really drunk. I don't know how that happened."

I do, but I decline to state. "Don't worry. We're having fun. I'll open another bottle, if you're game?"

"I better not, really." She tries to stand again and walks a step before crumpling to the ground.

"Erica!" I rush to her side and help her up. She's incoherent, and I think she hit her head on the floor. "Let's go to the couch."

She manages to walk with my help, a slow, painful walk. I deposit her, more roughly than I mean to but she doesn't notice. I feel for her pulse. It's slow, very slow.

I leave her on the couch and hurry back into the kitchen, scrubbing all the plates, wiping down everything: the table, the island, the refrigerator in the butler's pantry. I pull my gloves on and grab my salad bowl, tongs, and mason jar. Then I hurry out the front door and stash everything just outside in the bushes. I rush back inside and open a front hall coat closet, and as expected, the choices are vast. I pull on Erica's full-length raincoat, a designer brand and perfect for this evening.

By the time I'm back beside Erica on the couch, she's foaming at the mouth. I shake her, hard.

"Hey, Erica, wake up!" I slap her across the face and punch her arm. I kick her in the thigh. Nothing.

I slap her beautiful face again, harder, and blood begins to flow from her nose and mouth.

"I'm sorry, friend, but you shouldn't sleep with married men. It's not right," I say. I observe the damage and think it looks convincing. That she didn't put up much of a fight is a problem, but the two bottles of wine in the recycling bin could be the reason. I grab her under the arms and drag her off the couch. She lands, facedown, on the parquet floor; her left arm rests under the glass coffee table.

The coffee table is too tidy. I pick up the decorative heart made of white crystals and throw it onto the table. I watch as a spiderweb of cracks spreads across the glass.

I hurry back to the kitchen and wash the blood from my hands. Blood spatters cover my coat, but I'll deal with that at home.

"Good night, Erica," I say and hurry out through the fireplace-warmed courtyard for the last time. The beautifully crafted iron elements and arches really do make you feel like you're in the Mediterranean, just as the real estate agent promised in the listing description.

I walk briskly to Erica's car and wipe down the passenger side handle and the inside where I may have touched something, although I was careful and wearing gloves. I check the street. Nothing and nobody as usual. I carry my salad bowl and jog the few short blocks to the trailhead and freedom. Joanie Allen was never here, not that she ever existed. Erica was so gullible, so desperate to make a friend. And I would have liked her, except for her dangerous little habit of sleeping with my husband. Joanie needed to step in and make things right. And she did excellent work.

I reach my car, right where I left it, pull the uncomfortably tight ponytail holder off, and shake my hair free. I'm a blonde again, and we have more fun. I yank off the uncomfortable snap-on veneers and smile with relief. I remove the contact lenses while wiping the mole off my face with a tissue. It takes less than thirty minutes before I'm back home.

I didn't encounter a single other person all evening, besides Erica, of course. These gated communities are just so safe. I wonder if Jack has made it home yet? I'm sure he's in a hurry to see his girlfriend because he's just had a very long night at The Club trying to explain that there is nothing more than a coincidence between him starting as general manager and the theft ring.

Meanwhile, I'm home and have a chance to get myself and all my things cleaned up from the evening. Everything I wore tonight, including Erica's designer raincoat, will be shoved into a trash bag and added into the bag where I stashed the rest of the jimsonweed from my tower. I'll drive all of this to my inland storage facility tomorrow and dispose of it later this week at my favorite inland landfill. I don't think I'll need it anymore, but I'll keep the seeds here at the house, just in case. Did you know jimsonweed is one of the most poisonous plants found in North America? It's everywhere too. It grows on roads, in backyards. It's a weed. It's widespread. You've probably walked right past it before.

Turns out it even grows in hydroponic towers. Pretty little trumpet-shaped white flowers, toxic and beautiful. The seeds found inside the fruit are extra strong. The deadly effects of the plant were first discovered when they were mistakenly used by the Jamestown settlers with a deadly ending, thus the name jimsonweed. It's also called devil's trumpet, gypsum weed, moonflower, and thornapple.

Erica discovered firsthand the side effects from ingesting jimsonweed include tachycardia, dry mouth, dilated pupils, hallucinations, seizures, and death. It basically shuts down the central nervous system. Some people use it as a recreational drug to cause hallucinations, but it doesn't look that fun to me. When Jack drank my jimsonweed tea, he felt dizzy, tired, and a little sick. When he ate the salad two days before we left for our romantic trip to Utah, he had one-fourth the dose I gave to his girlfriend, and he still felt terrible for a couple of days, including our first day in Zion, although he tried to hide it.

I checked online to be sure, and I only needed to use twenty-five grams of the seeds to be deadly. That's just one and a half tablespoons. I added a little extra honey to my homemade salad dressing and in my homemade tea to cover the bitter taste.

Once again, I've fixed everything.

I climb into bed and pull out my notebook.

I'm worried about Jack again. I treated myself to lunch at The Club on Wednesday, and asked him to come by, to say hello. He did, finally, but he wouldn't stay and chat. He looked nervous, troubled, like something was wrong. I asked him how it was going with his new girlfriend, and he leaned forward and said, not well. I was shocked. I asked him if he needed anything, and he told me he would let me know.

He was scared, I know he was. He said she's violent, unhinged. They fight all the time, and she even throws things at him and drinks way too much. He doesn't know what he'll find when he comes home every night after work. He works so hard. He just wants peace, and now, he's found the opposite. He told me she threatened to hurt him if he leaves her. I told him I'm here for him, no matter what happens. I'll always love him, poor Jack. I really hope nothing terrible happens between them. I think he's just about to come back home to me, despite his girlfriend's demands. We shall see.

62
NOW

JACK

'm flooded with relief when Detective Donnelly calls and tells me to go home for the evening. Of course, the investigation continues.

"Jack, where are you going?" Sid asks as I walk out of my office. "Doesn't look like they're finished yet."

"They are with me."

"We need to inform the members what is happening."

I look at the ceiling and exhale. Of course, he's right. "Do you want it to come from me or the board?"

"Both of us," Sid says, and we walk into my office together. I type up what I know and hand him my computer to approve the email.

Dear members,
It is with regret we write to inform you The Club will be closed tomorrow and Saturday to all members and guests.

We understand this disruption is unexpected, but there have been a couple of thefts reported at The Club over the past two days or so, and we take these incidents very seriously. We hope you will understand we need to allow the police time to finish their investigation. We apologize to the members and guests affected and assure you whoever is responsible will be apprehended and prosecuted to the full extent of the law.

Very truly yours,

Mr. Jack Tingley   Mr. Sid Friday

Club Manager   Board Vice Chair

"Looks good. Send it. Say, could you give me a lift on your way home?" he asks.

There's nothing I'd rather do less.

"Sure."

I drop Sid off at his house, without so much as a thanks, and I floor it up the canyon road to Erica's house, fly down her street, and screech into her driveway. I've never been so glad to be home. I park out front, hurry through the courtyard, and slip the key in the front door. I notice she hasn't turned the alarm on, so she must be waiting up for me.

"Hey, Erica, I'm home." I'm still not used to all the space here, the hard surfaces, the rich wood and iron detailing, the soaring ceilings. When she doesn't answer, I take the steps two at a time racing up to our master bedroom. She likely fell asleep waiting for me.

She isn't in our bedroom though. A little hint of panic creeps into my mind, but I brush it off. It's been a long day. She's likely fallen asleep downstairs, watching TV.

But when I reach the family room, she's not there either. The kitchen is spotless, as if she didn't really have a friend over. But she said she did. My heart pounds with worry. Nothing makes sense. I run down the hallway to the garage and open the door. Her car is home. I pull out my phone and dial her number.

I listen as it rings somewhere in the house. I run back toward the entry hall and listen. But there is silence, my call rolled to voicemail. She is somewhere in the house.

"Erica, you're scaring me. Good hiding job, but you can come out now. I've had a really long day." I punch her number again and follow the sound of the ring toward the living room, a room we hardly ever use. I don't know why she'd be asleep there, but I hurry to find her with relief.

The first thing I see is Erica's open hand, palm up under the cracked glass coffee table. My mind tries to process what I'm looking at, but I can't. I rush to Erica's side, roll her over. There's so much blood, her face is a mess, and she's limp in my arms.

"Erica, wake up," I say. I punch 9-1-1 on my phone.

"What's your emergency?" the operator asks.

"It's my girlfriend. I just got home. She's been beaten up, I don't think she's breathing."

"Ok, I'm sending a squad to 3788 Black Dove Lane, correct?" she asks. "You need to start CPR. Do you know how?"

"Yes," I say and drop the phone. I pull Erica out from under the coffee table and begin chest compressions. "One, two, three, four, five, six, seven, eight, nine, ten." And then I breathe into her mouth, holding her bloody and broken nose. "One, two, three, four, five, six, seven, eight, nine, ten."

And I keep trying to save Erica until the paramedics arrive and take over before taking her away.

"Wait, I need to ride with you," I say, following them out the front door.

"Sir, you can follow us. We're headed to UCI Medical Center. We need to move now, she's barely alive," the paramedic says, slipping the gurney into the squad and flying off into the night.

Before I can find my car keys to leave, Detective Donnelly walks through the open front door. "What happened here, Jack?"

I grab my keys from the entry hall console and glance at my reflection in the mirror. I'm covered in Erica's blood.

"I don't know. I just got home. You know that. You've been with me all day, all night. I have to get to the hospital. You figure out who did this to my girlfriend."

I start to walk past him, but he stops me, hand up. "You left The Club at least twenty minutes ago. Did you and your girlfriend have a fight, Jack? I know it's been a long day. Did you take it out on her?" Donnelly's eyes are dark, threatening. His hand is behind his back. Does he intend to shoot me?

He has it all wrong. But I don't have time for this. "I need to be with Erica. Get out of my way," I say, then run to my car. "Find whoever did this."

"Oh, I will, Jack, I will!" Donnelly yells after me.

PART THREE

TWO WEEKS LATER

TUMBLING AFTER

63
NOW

JILL

The funeral is crowded, as it should be for someone as young and healthy and vibrant as Erica. And kind, of course. Erica was kind. And gullible, but so kind. Beside me, Michelle is holding Brad's hand, sobbing. Michelle didn't even know Erica for heaven's sake.

Of course, neither did I. In the short time that Joanie and Erica were friends, playing pickleball, beach walking and dining together, no one remembers seeing them together, even though poor Jack told the police they were best friends.

The police told me all about this when they came to see me at my home. I agreed to meet with them and take them around Jack's previous life, as long as they didn't touch anything. They promised to be careful. That it was just a fact-finding visit, to learn more about Jack Tingley from the person who knows him the best. When the detective—I think his name is Donnelly—saw my notebook out on my bedside table, he was very interested in reading it. I told him he couldn't take it. It was my private property and most of it was written during our marriage.

I have a feeling he's going to get a judge to make me share it with him. Whether I do is up to Jack.

"How will Jack handle this?" Michelle whispers to me.

"I'll be there for him, like always," I tell her. I tuck my hair behind my ear. My new blonde bob looks fresh and sexy, I've decided. And it should. The hairdresser in LA charged me an arm and a leg for the color and cut.

I look up front where Jack is sitting next to Erica's tear-soaked parents. They flew in from somewhere in the Midwest and seem overwhelmed and in shock. Jack acts like he's in charge of the funeral service, but that's awkward because many of the people here think he killed her.

He should have cleaned up before running into the hospital desperate to find Erica and looking like a serial killer. So many people took photos and video of him that night, he went viral: crazed eyes, covered in blood, running like a maniac, screaming Erica's name.

He was too late anyway. She died in the ambulance on the way to the hospital.

"Nice of you to be here, all things considered, Mrs. Tingley," Detective Donnelly says, shaking my hand. "Most spouses don't respect their husband's girlfriends enough to attend their funeral."

"Well, poor Jack needs all the support he can get, even if he doesn't deserve it," I say.

"Nice of you. Did you know Erica McCann?"

"No, of course not."

"Did you know her house burned down just a few months ago? A total loss?"

"Nope, don't know anything about that."

"It was ruled an accident, someone trying to keep warm at the beach during sunrise, but I'm not so sure now," Donnelly says. "See you around." He walks away headed toward the front of the room, toward Erica's white closed casket. I wonder why he is asking me all those questions. Erica was Jack's girlfriend, not mine, not really.

I watch the seats fill up with mourners, so many black-draped people. I see my favorite daughter, Maggie, swoop down the aisle and into her father's arms. I still haven't forgiven her for helping Jack move out while we were in Utah, but I haven't taken the time to focus on her.

I have time now.

I watch her back, stare at her, until she feels me watching, senses me in the room. She turns and spots me. I smile. She turns back around.

How dare she.

64
NOW

———

JACK

As much as I try to ignore the police and detectives sprinkled among the crowd filling the chapel, I can't.

They stare at me like I did this. Like I killed Erica.

Beside me, across the aisle, Erica's parents sob and cry, unable to speak to anyone. Thank goodness Maggie came home from school to be by my side. She squeezes my hand as the ceremony begins.

I don't listen. I think. Who would hurt Erica?

Detective Donnelly says it's always the husband. Well, I'm just a boyfriend. I told him Dean did it, and I think he believed me. Erica's ex-husband was jealous of our relationship and a control freak. I know they're trying to track him down.

Who would be capable of beating someone to death? Someone who was drunk, and the detectives tell me, likely passed out as she was being attacked? It's sick and twisted.

A voice in the back of my mind says Jill did this.

Jill stole from members and guests at The Club to frame you. And then, she killed Erica to ruin your happiness.

But could she? Would she?

She killed your parents, the voice says. But that was an accident, a fire meant to help protect me that burned out of control.

Jill could do this. But did she? Beside me, Maggie leans her head against my shoulder. I must protect her from Jill, no matter what it takes. And that means I cannot go to prison for killing Erica.

I'm lost in thought, struggling to find a way to prove I'm innocent when suddenly the priest's sermon is over. We all stand and sing a hymn, and the McCanns and Erica's casket disappear through a side door.

She's gone forever. And that thought breaks the dam inside, and I begin to cry uncontrollably for my best chance for a happy ending, my new true love. And for Ted, my best friend whose promising life was ended by me that night so long ago. And for my parents, may they rest in peace. It's all too much.

Maggie sits beside me and lets me cry as all the guests file out of the chapel.

All except one.

"Hello, Maggie," Jill says.

"Why are you here, Mom?" Maggie asks.

"To pay my respects obviously."

"But you don't respect anyone, certainly not Dad, not me, and not his girlfriend."

I wipe at my eyes and nose with my handkerchief. I know I'm going to need to intercede. "Thanks for coming, Jill."

"Of course. You're welcome. See how civil your dad and I are, Maggie? Why don't you two come over to the house for dinner tonight. I'm assuming you're still at that awful hotel, Jack?"

I nod. Ever since that night, I haven't been back to Erica's house. First it was a crime scene, and now, it's just haunted, ruined by an unknown killer. The McCanns will sell it soon, they told me. For the first few nights after Erica's death, The Club allowed me to sleep in my office. But the robberies are still unsolved, and my girlfriend has been murdered, so Sid knocked on my door one morning and told me I could keep my job for now, but I couldn't sleep here anymore.

I considered that a lucky break. I moved into a cheap motel just off the highway, ten miles from work. It's fine. It's clean.

I look at Maggie. I'll do whatever she'd like to do, but it might be a good idea to have us all back together again at home. Some days I think going to jail would be better than living with Jill again, but then I realize it is not a choice I get to make. She holds all the cards, my almost ex-wife. She can implicate me in Erica's murder; I'm sure she has the evidence tucked away somewhere along with a description in her precious notebook. I'd be locked away for life and Jill would be free to be Jill.

I need to protect my daughter.

Maggie looks at me. "Ok, one meal, but I'm not spending the night. I'm going back after dinner."

"Wonderful," Jill says. "I'll make something special. See you later."

Jill walks away with a spring in her step. I hope we made the right decision. I think about my parents. They would say we didn't.

65
NOW
———
JILL

And just like that, my family is together for dinner. Sure, it wasn't easy, but nothing worth having is easy to get.

Jack is coming home. To me. Maggie will only stay for a short time and will disappear back up north, out of sight, out of mind. I hope she doesn't try to stir me up. I'm just not in the mood.

"What can I do?" Maggie asks, appearing in the kitchen in a UC Santa Cruz T-shirt, no bra, and sweatpants. I wonder if she'll fly back to college looking like that.

"Actually, can you set the table?" I ask, turning back to my salad waiting to be tossed in its favorite wooden bowl. Although I still have some seeds left, I decide tonight I will serve a simple, healthy salad, no added surprises for anyone.

I could pinch myself I'm so happy. We look like the perfect family, even if Jack has dark circles under his eyes and barely smiles. He'll get better, it just takes time. In fact, looking at him now, sitting in his favorite chair in the family room, I'm reminded of how he looked, and acted, after the accident with Ted. It's as if all the life was sucked out of him.

And now, after poor Erica's untimely death, he's drained again.

"Can I bring you anything, Jack?" I call to him from the kitchen.

"No, I'm fine. Thank you." He is staring at the television. I hope it's not the news, although the coverage of Erica McCann's unsolved murder has died down at least. It used to be breaking news nationally and obsessively covered locally. Beautiful woman, gorgeous home, gated community—nothing bad ever happens to people in The Club and its community.

That's true, if they aren't husband stealers like Erica was.

"Table is all set. Call me when dinner's ready," Maggie says. "I'll be in my room."

Of course. Maggie is either in her room, eating, or gone. It works for me, and her. We're not compatible, but at least we both know it. I think about my mom for a minute and wonder if she misses me. I'm sure she's heard all the gossip by now, from Ben and especially Rhonda, about what a sinner I am, and how I left my husband behind at the national park. But Mom hasn't reached out. Nobody has. I suppose that's for the best. Once banished, always banished.

The water is boiling, so I slip the linguine into the pot. I've chopped tomatoes, basil, and garlic for a simple sauce. The salad and dressing are ready, and a loaf of sourdough bread is waiting on the table. I should open some wine. Yes, that's a nice touch.

I'm uncorking a nice pinot when Maggie reappears.

"Dinner's almost ready," I tell her and return to the wine bottle.

"Mom, are you trying to frame Dad for Erica's murder?"

I pull the cork out and stare at my daughter. "Don't be ridiculous."

"I read this, well the last few entries, and that was enough." She holds up my notebook.

Did I leave it out? "Give me that," I say. "That is personal property, my diary. You have no right to read any of it."

I lunge at her, but she leaps away.

"You've been setting him up, writing about fights between him and Erica. They didn't fight." Maggie yells, "Dad, come in here."

"Give me my notebook," I scream and charge her, knocking Maggie to the ground and grabbing my notebook. "I mean, even if you take it, I've got it all backed up on the cloud. You don't think I'm stupid do you?"

"Jill, my god, what are you doing?" Jack rushes to Maggie's side, helping her up from the floor.

"She's horrible, Dad. You have to stay away from her," Maggie says. She's shaking. I scared her.

I'm glad.

"You're the one who should leave, Maggie. Go back to school." I want to say get the hell out of here, but I don't. I'm her mom and that would be rude. Oh whatever. I yell, "Get the hell out of here!"

"Jill, stop it," Jack says and pulls Maggie closer to him. "What is going on in here? Why are you two fighting?"

"I found Mom's little secret notebook," Maggie says. "She's written all this stuff about you that's not true. How you steal things for fun, and how you and Erica fought all the time."

Jack turns to me. I hold my notebook close to my chest.

"Did you give the detectives permission to read that?" he asks. His eyes are sad, his voice weak and scratchy.

I stare at him. He really has fallen apart since he left me. What a stupid decision on his part. I look down at my notebook. "No, I haven't given it to them, not yet."

"Oh my god, Mom," Maggie says.

"Why, Jill? Why are you doing this to me?" Jack asks.

I look at him and smile. "You know the answer, handsome." I can't believe he can't understand that I only want one thing. Just one thing. He's staring at me shaking his head.

"You left me," I say. "All you had to do was stay."

66

NOW

JACK

Maggie insists on taking an Uber, even though I offer to drive her to the airport.

"Dad, I'm fine. I don't want anything from her, I don't love her, I've worked through it all. She can't hurt me anymore," she says as we wait outside for her ride. "But she can hurt you."

"She won't, honey. You heard her. All she wants is for me to come back to her. Why would she hurt me when that's what she wants?"

"You can't move back in. Dad, don't even think of it."

"You read the notebook. You know what she's capable of saying, writing, about me."

"Yes. It's horrible."

"The only way to keep her from saying any of that to the police is to keep her happy," I say. I know it's likely Jill who killed Erica, but I can't bear to tell my daughter that her mother is a killer, especially since I know I'll likely have to go back to her. I take a deep breath. "It's the only way, at least until Erica's killer is caught, and the jewelry thief. It could be the same person. It's just not me. You believe me, don't you?"

"Dad, of course. But I don't trust Mom, not at all."

"I know. But I need you to keep quiet about all of this. We don't want a court case dragging all of us down. Your life is just beginning. You need to leave here and move forward. I'm so sorry I didn't leave your mom sooner, but as you can tell, it's tricky. But you're free now."

"But what about you? You need help."

"No, I don't. This is my mess. I'm sorry I even asked for your help moving my stuff out. It was wrong, and weak. I should have just handled Jill on my own."

Maggie looks at me with tears in her eyes. "I love you, Dad. You didn't do anything wrong. But I understand. I won't say anything to anyone. You need to be careful," she says and gives me a big hug.

"I'm safe, as long as I stay with her, honey. Don't worry. Do you feel safe in your new apartment?"

"It's like a fortress, Dad. The safest on campus. Thank you," Maggie says. "Besides, it's not me she wants, she never has, as we both know by now."

We stand side by side, staring at the house across the street, lost in thought.

A car pulls up to the curb, and Maggie checks her app. "It's my ride. If you do move back in, I'll only be able to see you when you come to visit me. I'm never coming back home again."

"I agree. Maybe, one day, I can move up to Northern California too. No matter what, I'll be visiting often. You won't be able to shake me. I love you, and I'm so proud of you." I kiss her on the forehead, and then she slips into the car and she's gone.

A wave of relief washes over me. At least one of us is safe.

I walk up to the front door with dread. Instead of going back inside with Jill, I wish I could drive home to my hotel. But I can't. I am the only one who can keep her in line. And her silence is the only way I stay out of prison. I know the police are eyeing me as their prime suspect.

The last thing I need is for my almost ex-wife to confirm their narrative. I take a deep breath and walk inside, closing the door behind me.

"Is she gone?" Jill asks, meeting me at the door, offering a glass of red wine.

"She is." Her contempt for her only child infuriates me once again. "Thanks for the wine."

"Sure," she says. "She really knows how to push my buttons."

I follow Jill back to the kitchen, biting my tongue, a new plan forming in my mind. I have no other choice. "Smells great. Your signature pasta, I see."

"Yes, just for you. I hope you're hungry."

"You know, I really am." I feel like I'm a character in a sitcom or something, carefully selecting my words, dancing around Jill like she's a toxic cloud. She *is* a toxic cloud. And she needs to die. She does.

"Since it's just the two of us, I'll light the candles," she says. I watch her on her phone. She turns on the house music system, playing Frank Sinatra. Then she dims the lights. "Romantic, right? This is what I imagine every night being like."

"Wow," I say and follow her to the table. I decide to wait until we're settled and eating before I ask her what she wrote in the notebook, and most importantly, why. For now, I'm going to enjoy some good food, good wine, and pretend I'm with someone else. I take a bite of pasta. It's good.

I try to imagine sitting down with Erica, but the horrible image of her bloody face jumps into my mind. I look up from my plate.

"You killed Erica, didn't you?" I ask, standing and walking to her side of the table.

Jill isn't eating. Instead, she's staring at me. "Don't be silly."

In a moment, I'm on her, my hands wrapped around her neck. Her eyes bulge and she struggles against me, choking sounds coming from her mouth. I squeeze tighter and look into her eyes. And then I let go.

Jill slumps to the ground, gasping for air, her hands massaging her neck. "How dare you."

"How dare you," I say, staring down at her.

"Help me up," she says, and I offer my hand. She walks to the kitchen, takes a green linen napkin out of the drawer, and ties it around her neck. She walks back to the table and sits down. I join her.

"That better not ever happen again, Jack," she says, stirring the pasta on her plate with her fork.

"I lost control. You pushed me too far and I snapped. It's your fault."

She shakes her head, staring at me.

I wipe my mouth with my napkin, afraid I have sauce on my face. I don't. "What? Say something."

Before she can answer, there is a loud knock on the door.

67
NOW

JILL

I've worked so hard to get here. And now, of course, our perfect moment, the first one in a very long time, is ruined. First, Jack tries to kill me, but he couldn't handle strangling me. That takes too long and it's too intimate. You must stare at your victim as the life slowly ebbs out, for minutes. He couldn't handle it, I knew that. Still, my neck is sore.

I'm going to kill whoever is at the front door.

"I'll answer it," I say. Jack looks so startled, so guilty, frankly, he should stay seated.

I open the door and reveal Detective Donnelly. "Hope I'm not bothering you, ma'am, but I need to ask you a couple questions. May I come in?"

As usual, he smells like mothballs and still needs to trim his ear hair. Do I want him inside my home? No. Do I have a choice? No.

"My husband and I were just enjoying a romantic meal together," I say. "But you can come in if it won't take long."

"Your husband?" he asks, stepping into the foyer. "Jack Tingley?"

"Yes, he is my only husband."

"You're divorced, right?"

"No, nothing is finalized. We have reconnected after all. I've dropped the proceedings. We're meant to be together." It would be hard not to notice the Frank Sinatra playing, the dimmed lights, the smell of garlic in the air. "I need to get back to my dinner, Detective."

"Sure, whatever." He opens his notebook and pulls out a grainy black and white photo. "Do you recognize this woman?"

I take the photo and pretend to study it. It's me, of course, with red hair in a high ponytail and big sunglasses, dressed as Joanie Allen, riding in the passenger seat of Erica's Range Rover. We're stopped at a stop sign at the top of Erica's street. Whatever neighbor has pointed a camera at the stop sign should be arrested for invasion of privacy. Unacceptable. The Club should take action.

"No, should I?" I ask.

"She looks a lot like you, actually."

"No, not really. She has a fuller face. She's younger. And she has darker hair. Who is she?"

"A friend of the deceased. Since Jack is here, do you mind if I show him the photo?"

"Tonight? Again, Detective, we are having a date. Our first chance to really connect after all that's happened."

"I'm sure he won't mind. If he's telling the truth, this woman was the last person to see Erica McCann alive. He'll want to help us find her, and now we have a photo," he says. "Mr. Tingley?"

Jack walks into the foyer as if he'd been listening in all along. "Good evening, Detective. How can I help you?"

Donnelly hands him the photo. "Do you recognize this woman? This is Joanie, Erica's friend. We haven't been able to locate her, but we do have this photo now."

I watch Jack stare at the photo. He swallows. He looks at me. "Is that you?"

"What? No, it isn't," I say. My cheeks are hot and my throat is dry from being strangled. "She's much younger. Erica's age. Why on earth would I be hanging out with your girlfriend, Jack? That's absurd."

"We all think it's you, Mrs. Tingley. Why were you going to Ms. McCann's home on the night she died?" Detective Donnelly asks. "You should know we have experts who are enhancing this photo, and with facial recognition techniques as good as they are these days, well it won't be long until we can say conclusively that it's you."

"Don't say another word. Detective, I'm going to need you to leave now."

"Actually, I think I might need to take you down to the station," Donnelly says.

"No, I won't go. I'm calling a lawyer. This is harassment." I pivot and walk away from him, hurrying into the kitchen. "Jack, get in here."

Jack appears in the kitchen, deer in the headlights.

"You were Joanie?" Jack asks. He reaches for the kitchen island behind him. "Her pickleball friend? Her new best friend?"

I lean into him and whisper in his ear. "Let me be clear, Jack, you need to tell the detective that's not me in the photo, understand? Or I'll go get the notebook."

68
THEN

JILL

While Jack enjoyed some guy time with his friends at the fall formal, I was able to slip away and confront his good buddy, Ted. I didn't, of course, tell him what I thought of him and his undermining ways. No, I had a different plan.

But I knew what he had been whispering in Jack's ear, almost from the minute we began dating. Ted told him I wasn't good enough for him, that something was "off" with me. Yes, I heard that one. Jack listened to Ted. They were best friends, since kindergarten or something. So knowing all of that, and also knowing that Ted and Mr. and Mrs. Tingley were close, it was obvious I needed to get rid of Ted.

Sally was so helpful. She and Ted had quite a tumultuous relationship, one that was bound to end sooner or later. She was a debutante, with proper breeding, and Ted liked that.

He also liked to brag about how her family was so prominent. He did so, in front of me and Jack, just to bring me down.

I found Sally in line for the bathroom inside the Lake Arrowhead home.

"Oh, there you are," I told her, joining her in line and ignoring the groans from the girls behind her.

"This line is taking forever," she said.

"I know about another bathroom upstairs. Follow me. And here, have some of my drink."

She did. She took a big gulp, silly Sally. As we climbed the stairs to the second floor, she began swaying a bit.

"I don't feel so good," she said. "I need to lay down."

"Oh no, ok, let me find you a bathroom, and a bedroom," I said, helping her walk down the hall. I pushed open the first door at the top of the stairs and almost carried Sally inside, then closed the door behind us. I positioned her on the bed on her side, just in case, slipped a pillow under her head, and hurried out of the room.

My first jimsonweed experiment. I hoped, for Sally's sake, I'd used the right dose.

When I made it back outside, the party was still in full swing. I'd barely taken a few steps toward the dance floor when Ted grabbed my arm.

"Hey, Jill, have you seen Sally? Somebody told me you were with her inside. Is everything ok? I can't find her."

I looked him in the eye. "No. Everything isn't fine, I'm afraid. She's really angry with you. She is drunk too, and told me she is walking home."

"What? No? She can't, what is she thinking? Why didn't you come find me?" Ted said, his eyes flashing.

"I'm telling you now. If you hurry, you can find her. She's following the road, that's all she'd say. I couldn't make her stop." I swiped at a fake tear under my eye. "Here. Drink some water and sober up. Please, go find her, it's dangerous out there."

Ted considered the red cup in my hand, grabbed it, and began to spring toward the lake house and the dark country road beyond.

I searched the crowd and spotted Jack holding court at the bar. He waved to me, and we met in the middle of the party, under the twinkling party lights.

"Hey, handsome," I said, slipping my arm through his.

"Hey, gorgeous. I know you're having fun, but I have to go. I'm sorry, but I have to get a good score on the LSATs tomorrow afternoon or my parents will murder me."

"I know. Let's go," I said. "I'm happy as long as I'm with you."

"And I love being with you too. Let's go!"

We reached his BMW without too much delay, and before I knew it, we were driving down the dark, windy road beside the lake.

Did I know Ted would appear, stumbling along the road, in a frantic search for Sally, who was passed out in an upstairs bedroom of the lake house where I'd left her?

No, but I hoped we'd encounter him. And we did. Violently. Fatally.

He wore a dark suit, and the night was moonless with thick fog working its way up from the lake.

Ted was impossible to see on the road until the last moment. I do remember spotting the red cup in his hand.

I know he didn't feel much pain, what with all the alcohol he'd ingested, and my extra dose of jimsonweed in his water. I couldn't tell Jack about that part though, of course not, even though I knew it would bring him some comfort.

Poor Jack just had to suffer with the knowledge he was a murderer. But really, as I told him, it was Ted's fault for being out there in the first place. If we hadn't run him over, the truck would have.

I did check for a pulse that night—it was faint, but I lied about that—and picked up the red cup and tossed it in the back seat. I'd demanded that Jack let me drive. He was distraught, unfit to operate heavy machinery.

Meanwhile, I was stone-cold sober.

As I pulled away, well, I must admit, despite everything poor Jack was going through, I was relieved. The enemy number one to our lifelong happiness had met his just end. I'd decided I'd do anything to keep Jack and me together. And I have. I fixed everything.

69
NOW

JACK

I stare at Jill, unable to comprehend what is happening.

"You befriended her, and then you killed her?" I whisper.

"I did it for you, for us, just like I've fixed so many other things, from the very beginning," Jill whispers. "Ted, well, there was a reason he was out on that road the night of the formal, you know?"

"No." My pulse quickens. I feel ill.

"Yes, handsome. Teddy was undermining us, me. He had to go. But let's focus on tonight. Now, here's what you're going to do. You're going back out to the foyer, and you will tell the detective that's not me in the photo. Because even if it is, our attorney will suppress it. I was at The Club a lot that week, plenty of times to be photographed, remember? Besides, I don't wear my hair in a ponytail. I can't. It's too short."

I stare at Jill and realize she's cut her hair. A chill rolls down my spine.

"No, Jill, it's over. You need to turn yourself in. You aren't well. Please. You need help."

"The help I need is in the form of marital privilege. You keep quiet about my deeds, and I'll keep quiet about yours. As long as we're married, we can't be forced to testify against each other."

My head is spinning. There is still a detective in the foyer. My wife murdered my girlfriend, violently. My wife somehow got my best friend to walk on a dark road where she knew I'd run him over. My wife killed my parents. My wife is a monster.

"I haven't done anything wrong. I don't need privilege."

Jill tips her head back and laughs. "Let's start with you just tried to kill me. Oh, and there's the loot in your car."

"What?" I ask, head spinning. "What are you talking about?"

"All the stolen items from The Club. They're all out in the garage, inside your car." Her ice-blue eyes dance in the dimmed light.

"No, that can't be."

"I know. And you really seem to like that job, sticky fingers and all. Do you want me to take the detective out there for a look-see?"

"No. Please."

"Or I could hand him my notebook. That would clear up so much for him. I don't want to do that, Jack. I'd rather just stay married. Be partners in crime, so to speak. We don't want to turn into witnesses against each other, do we? Can you imagine, both of us in prison? Maggie an orphan. Horrible.

I mean, think of all the terrible things that could happen to a young woman alone in the world. And, Jack, bruises are developing around my neck. That would be awkward to show the detective, yes?"

I'm never going to get away from her. Not ever.

"You will leave Maggie alone forever. I need you to promise me that," I say.

"I don't care about her. Fine. She's dead to me."

"I'll go tell the detective it doesn't look like you," I say.

Jill smiles. "And tell him to go away. He's ruining our dinner."

"Yes, of course."

"And I'll take care of the jewelry and other treasures hidden in your car. Maybe we can even go on a fabulous vacation. You deserve it after all this heartache you've been through."

"And the notebook?" I ask.

"I'll get rid of it too," she says.

I don't believe her though. She's held that stupid thing over my head for more than twenty years. "You won't."

"I will. As long as you make me a promise. You know what I want. You. Forever."

I take a deep breath. "I'll be right back."

I walk into the foyer and find Detective Donnelly has made himself at home in the living room. He stands slowly as I approach the chair.

"Your wife is nuts, isn't she?" he says. "We're going to break this case, one way or another. Your help is essential."

"I think it was Erica's ex-husband Dean who killed her, I really do," I say. "That photo wasn't of Jill. I would know.

We've been together forever. So, unless there's anything else you need tonight, I should let you get back to work. We really need to find that guy."

Detective Donnelly shakes his head. "We'll find him, don't worry. And we'll make a positive ID of the woman in the photo. It's Mrs. Tingley. I'd bet my career on it."

"You shouldn't bet against Jill," I say. "Good night, Detective."

As I watch him walk away and disappear into the night, I wish I could trade places. But I can't. The only thing I can do is rebuild my arsenal against Jill. It's my only protection, really. My form of a notebook, I suppose, my recordings of her confessions. I'd be much further ahead if I hadn't lost so much content when my phone tumbled away into the canyon.

I'll never forget the moment when I set up my new phone and realized Jill had disconnected the sync to the cloud. It's infuriating how she's always one step ahead. I lost everything I'd recorded on the trip. I'll try to get her to talk again tonight. Still, even as I put my phone on record, I know I'll never have enough to leave.

I made my bed all those years ago, and now, I am going to have to lie in it forever.

70
NOW

JACK

I walk into the kitchen to find Jill heating our pasta bowls in the microwave.

"Bravo!" she says and claps her hands. "Well done. I'm so proud of you."

I try to find something to say, but I can't. Instead, I walk to the counter and refill our wineglasses. The microwave beeps.

"Ok, let's try this again, hopefully without further interruptions," Jill says, carrying our bowls to the kitchen table. "Now, after your attempted murder of me, where were we?"

Somehow, I'm still hungry. I take a bite of pasta. My phone lights up with a text. Maggie is on the plane about to take off. I text her: I love you. Fly safe. Text when you land!

I feel Jill's stare. "It's Maggie. She's taking off."

"Excellent. She won't bother us for a while either, then."

"No, she won't," I say. I make sure my phone is recording and slip it onto my lap.

"This is so nice. Just the two of us, intimate, private. We can talk about anything, handsome, because we're married and we will be, forever. So tell me, what's on your mind?"

71
NOW

JILL

I smile at my husband sitting across the table from me, where he should be.

"The pasta is really good," he says. He won't hold eye contact.

I hope he isn't being obstinate. I don't want to have to start poisoning him again. But I will. "No, besides my great cooking. What are you thinking about?"

"I'm, well, wondering what happens next, I guess."

"What happens next is I pawn the items *you* stole from The Club, and you and I go on a fabulous vacation. Maybe Italy? Pasta all day, every day."

"Ok, but then what?" He's almost finished his pasta. I slide my bowl to him. I'm not hungry at all.

"I haven't planned out all the rest of the years of our lives, but I think we'll move. What with the mayor thing, The Club stuff, and Erica, well, let's just say we have a bit of an image problem. Need a new start. Maybe Hawaii. There are so many country clubs there."

"Jill, no more," he says.

"I mean for you to work at, nothing more," I say. "What do you think of Hawaii?"

"I think Donnelly will come after us. I don't think he's going to let this go. Because if there is no Joanie, and if her ex-husband isn't found, which he probably won't be, that leaves us. We are the last two people who saw Erica alive."

"Why won't Erica's ex-husband be found?" I ask, tilting my head. Jack drops his gaze to the pasta.

"He just won't be," he says.

"Oh my god, did you kill her ex?" I ask, truly surprised for once. "How did you do it? This is fascinating."

Jack smiles. "I'm pleading the fifth. Let's focus on Erica's murder, shall we?"

"Fun. You killed him. I'd love to hear more. But sure, back to Erica. I wasn't there. Everything I do is to protect you, Jack," I say. "Stop worrying. They don't have any evidence to link you to her murder. But of course, I do."

"That's because I didn't do it. You did," he says.

"Are you ready for some coffee, tea?" I stand and walk into the kitchen.

I hope we aren't going to go over this ad nauseum like we did with the Ted thing. The past is the past, what's done is done. I don't think I can handle rehashing Erica's demise over and over again. And now that I know what he's capable of, I need to be a little more cautious. Jack's a murderer too, it seems. I was right all along. We do belong together. I'll make him some special tea so he'll sleep.

"Sure. And then I need to get going."

"You're not going to sleep at that hotel anymore. Not when we have a whole house right here. Move back in. I insist."

Jack rests his head on his chin. "Why not."

Well, that's not the spirit I was looking for. "Try again? With a little more enthusiasm?"

He leans back in the chair, closes his eyes. "Sounds great!"

"Better," I say. "You know, we could start to have fun together again. It's possible now that your distraction is out of the way."

He grimaces when I say it, but he knows I'm right.

"Can we please just not talk about Erica? Please," he says. "The nightmares are back."

"I don't want to ever talk about her again. And of course the nightmares are back, Jack," I tell him. The teakettle whistles. I turn off the burner and pour the water over my special tea. "We need to work on rewriting the endings, talking through what you're feeling. All of those things we started on our trip. But then, it was cut short. By you."

"Right," he says.

I place the tea in front of him and sit down.

"Thanks. So, were you going to kill me, push me over the rim, leave me forever with the hoodoos?" he asks. He takes a sip of tea.

I smile. That seems so long ago. My anger has subsided considerably now that I've fixed things. "I don't know. Perhaps the thought crossed my mind."

"Do you still want to kill me? Tell me the truth."

Right now, no. If he stays in line, never. "I'm so happy you're home, of course I don't want to kill you. And you? Do you still want to kill me?"

"Not at the moment. And you'd never hurt Maggie?"

"I've dreamed of it, believe me, but I made a promise to you, and to her, when she was born. I can't take out of the world the only thing I've put into it." I take off the napkin I tied around my neck so he can see the developing bruises. "She's safe, but it's better if she stays away. Wouldn't want her to see the real us."

He nods, covering his yawn with his hand. "I'm really tired. I haven't slept in ages."

"You'll sleep well tonight, handsome, I will make sure of it."

He looks at me, alarmed. "Did you put something in the tea? I feel dizzy."

"Don't worry so much. Come on, let's make you comfortable in the guest room. I don't want to rush things."

"That's a good idea," he says, slurring a bit. "Take things one step at a time."

The next thing I know, he's passed out, head on the table, snoring.

He'll be fine. And I will be too.

Jack's home.

I slip my hand onto his lap and grab his phone. He was recording me again. I was afraid of that. I delete all the files. He is going to need to be more honest, or else.

72

NOW

JACK

I wake up at the kitchen table with a stiff neck and back. Outside, the sky is the light blue of morning. I stand up and fill a glass with water, then chug it down, trying to clear my foggy head.

I can't believe I'm back home.

With Jill.

I pull out my phone and try to find the audio recordings I made last night. The first, when Detective Donnelly was waiting in the foyer, the second, later, when we were talking here at the kitchen table. They've been deleted.

Jill.

I'm back where I started. Jill won't let me live a life without her, I know that now. I'm trapped. And it's my fault. I start to allow myself to remember how great it was with Erica, but I stop. That was an illusion of perfection and happiness. This is my reality. Maybe it's karma for killing Erica's ex. No, he was a bad guy; he needed to disappear. It's surprising to me how easily I can justify a murder.

Maybe I am more like Jill than I thought.

"Good morning, sleepyhead," Jill says, appearing in the kitchen full of sunshine and smiles. "I've taken the liberty of calling you in sick for work today, and for the rest of the week. I visited my favorite pawn shop, and I am flush with cash. Our flight leaves this afternoon. We're going to have such a fabulous time. Sound good?"

"No, Jill, I should go to work, keep my regular routine," I say, standing and stretching. I cannot believe I slept an entire night and part of this day at the kitchen table.

"Nonsense. I won't take no for an answer. You need to get some sunshine in your life," she says, bustling around the kitchen like a vision of suburban perfection. She's even wearing an apron.

"How'd you sleep?" she asks. "I bet you didn't have any nightmares!"

"You're right about that," I say. "Is that fresh squeezed orange juice?"

"It is. And I have a sausage frittata from the bakery too, just need to heat it up. Getting into the Italian spirit, preparing for our trip. Go get dressed and pack a few things. The car service picks us up in an hour."

Why not?

"Ok, sure, I'll go pack. Thanks, you know, for everything. For not killing me. I want you to know I heard you loud and clear last night. Right up until the time I passed out because you drugged me."

"Yes, well you got a good night's sleep. But I hope you mean it. Do you? Because you keep messing up." She tilts her head with a smile. "This will be your last chance. You better not try to kill me again. It would be a mistake."

I believe her. As I head upstairs to pack, I tell myself to be thankful for another day, no matter the circumstances. I look out the window and notice one of the detective's officers parked in an undercover vehicle across the street. I wonder what they'll think when we head to the airport.

It's too bad I'm the only one who can help them find what they're looking for.

As you know by now, my wife won't let that happen.

I need a reset button. I need a change of heart. I need to accept my fate. Until I can change things. I think about the $150,000 in an offshore account. Jill thinks she took the city money to frame me, but she was in way over her head. I grabbed it and deleted the electronic trail. It's my other safety net. I may use it to hire a private investigator when we get home from this trip.

I think about Jill, about all she's capable of doing, all that she is. I see her smile, the one that drew me to her all those years ago. I can fall in love with her again, I tell myself. I will try, for real this time, to reconnect. As Jill kept telling me, there really is no other choice. It's fall back in love with my wife or lose my life.

73
NOW

JILL

The Mediterranean Sea sparkles below us as we sit on cushioned lounge chairs side by side. The Amalfi Coast was my idea, a relaxing haven of wealth and good food, la dolce vita so to speak. It's like a second honeymoon for Jack and me.

The resort exudes sophistication, with elegant architecture that blends seamlessly into the dramatic cliffs of the coast. The view is breathtaking—picturesque villages with colorful buildings cascading down the hillsides, framed by lush greenery and vibrant bougainvillea. It's almost like Laguna Beach, to be honest, minus the ever-lurking detective.

Jack looks better already, tanned and happy. His nightmares have subsided, and now he looks every bit the part of a wealthy, spoiled American. A gentle sea breeze keeps the temperature perfect, and the sound of the waves lapping against the rocky shoreline is so calming.

"Would you like a glass of Prosecco, handsome?" I ask. "I'm going to go ask the waiter for one."

"Sure, that would be great. And maybe something to snack on?"

"Of course, whatever you want." I kiss him on the cheek. He didn't flinch, which is good. He's getting used to my touch again, and that makes me happy.

As I stand, I notice a couple sitting in the chairs next to ours. She's young, maybe late twenties, dripping in jewels: huge wedding ring, diamond-encrusted watch, sparkling diamond studs in her ears. The designer bathing suit and bag are the same brand, ultra expensive.

I smile as I watch her and her new husband settling in. Fate has brought me our new mark. I'm so excited.

"Jill, what are you doing?" Jack asks. He is now sitting up in his lounge chair. Watching me watch the newlyweds.

"Just admiring the young couple."

"Don't you dare, we're not having that kind of fun anymore, remember."

"I'm just going to go get those glasses of Prosecco. I'll be right back," I say and walk away, stopping in front of the newlyweds.

"You two must be on your honeymoon," I say, all sugar and spice and everything nice.

"We are," says the young diamond-encrusted newlywed wife. "It's gorgeous here. We just arrived. How about you two?"

She looks over at Jack. Jack watches us from his lounge chair. He gives a small wave.

"It's our second honeymoon, yes. We'll be here all week. You?"

"Us too. I'm Sarah and this is Sam."

This is perfect. "I'm Jill and that's Jack!"

"Like the nursery rhyme," she says.

"Just like it," I say. "I'm heading to the bar, would you like me to bring you anything?"

Sarah smiles and stands up. "I'll go with you. Be right back, hon."

I glance at Jack. He's shaking his head, warning me. So cute.

Beside me, Sarah is babbling away about pasta, limoncello, and how cheap everything is compared to home. I don't care, but I pretend to. Her wedding ring alone could float us for half a year.

Proseccos in hand, we walk back to the pool area, taking our seats next to our respective husbands after making plans to meet for dinner that night. Poor Sarah explained her husband just doesn't talk that much and she's getting bored. On their honeymoon! I'll give them something to talk about.

"You need to stop it," Jack says as I hand him the Prosecco, the little bubbles dancing in his glass. "I know what you're doing. Maybe we should leave, change hotels, so you won't be tempted. That's just too easy. And they're on their honeymoon. It's just not right."

"It is. They have too much, too young. Anyway, we're having dinner with them tonight, and then, yes, we will be leaving once I get what I need. Don't worry, handsome."

Jack sighs and takes a big drink of the sparkling wine. Accepting his fate, perhaps? Or maybe not. All I know is Jack is under control now, and there isn't another woman in his life to distract him, not anymore. We will fall back in love, I'm sure of it. We just need time alone to reconnect. We will protect each other, keep each other's secrets until death do we part.

And, of course, have a little fun along the way. I'm so happy.

The End

ACKNOWLEDGEMENTS

With every novel I write, I am reminded that story-telling is never a solitary journey. It takes a village of passionate, supportive, and inspiring individuals who breathe life into the process, and I am endlessly grateful for all of you.

To my readers and fans—your support means the world to me. Thank you for spending your time in the world I've created and for sharing your excitement, thoughts, and emotions. Your posts, reviews, and messages, whether on Instagram or other social platforms, have given me countless moments of joy and inspiration. You're the heartbeat of every book, and I couldn't do this without you.

To my phenomenal team at Penzler Publishing and the Scarlet imprint—Otto Penzler, Luisa Cruz Smith, Charles Perry, Julia O'Connell, Will Luckman, and every incredible person who pours their talent into making this dream a reality—thank you for believing in my stories and elevating them with your expertise and care. I feel incredibly fortunate to work alongside such dedicated professionals who understand the craft and magic of suspense.

Thank you as well to the amazing Kathie Bennett of Magic Time who has elevated my tour this year, and I'm forever grateful. Megan Beatie—you're a fantastic publicist. Thank you. And Suzy Leopold, we've been together since the beginning. So nice to have you on my team. Speaking of teams, I am part of a great one: the Killer Author Club, a biweekly show and podcast hosted by Kimberly Belle, Heather Gudenkauf, and me. Check it out: www.killerauthorclub.com

To my family, and especially my husband, Harley—thank you for being my anchor and my cheerleader. Your unwavering support, patience, and above-and-beyond devotion make everything possible. You keep me grounded while encouraging me to chase the wildest of dreams, and I am endlessly grateful for you.

To my incredible manager and producing partner, Liza Fleissig of Liza Royce Associates, and her remarkable partner, Ginger Harris-Dontzin—you have made a profound impact on my career in ways I will never be able to fully express. And we've only just begun. Your dedication, wisdom, and belief in me have been a gift beyond measure. From the bottom of my heart, thank you.

To everyone who has played a part in this journey—whether in small moments or monumental ways—thank you for making this novel possible. You've not only helped shape the story but shaped my life as a writer. I'd love to keep in touch. You can find me on social media and at www.kairarouda.com

KAIRA ROUDA is an award-winning, *USA Today* and Amazon Charts bestselling author of contemporary fiction that explores what goes on beneath the surface of seemingly perfect lives. She is a founding member of the Killer Author Club, a bi-monthly live show supporting authors. She is also a member of Sisters in Crime, Mystery Writers of America, Women's Fiction Author Association, and the International Thriller Writers Association. She lives in Southern California with her family.

KairaRouda.com | Instagram/X: @KairaRouda
Facebook: KairaRoudaBooks